VALOR

Emily Bates

authorHOUSE®

AuthorHouse™
1663 Liberty Drive
Bloomington, IN 47403
www.authorhouse.com
Phone: 1 (800) 839-8640

Published by AuthorHouse   04/27/2018

ISBN: 978-1-5462-4049-5 (sc)
ISBN: 978-1-5462-4048-8 (e)

Library of Congress Control Number: 2018905219

Print information available on the last page.

The story of Brave Jovan

Chapter 1

Jovan's breath was like chalk dust against the onyx sky. Breathing in and out was hard, his lungs full of the heavy air and his heart beating like an anvil. Today was the end of it all. It was finally all over.

Jovan and his soldiers had been fighting a battle for the past three months. On and off again, they had been attacked; and they had fought back just as many times. The battle of Januvia, and his town of Hawthorne had fought a tiring battle that was finally all over. Jovan had been weakened and scared and beat down, but he had ran face-first into the battle, and he had swung his sword right at the heart of the enemy, and he knew that he had won.

Jovan had cried a battle cry that day that all the town could hear. All men had stopped to look at him, and they, too, knew; the fight was over, and they had won.

Jovan never looked back at falling soldiers or spilled blood. He tried not to think about the things that haunted his mind, things he had seen and done, that he never wanted to speak of again. Jovan never thought about the baying of horses or the crying of men. They sometimes echoed to him in his dreams; but he always came away with an image of himself, bloody sword raised, as he faced an empty battlefield. It was a rush of poison in his veins, toxic to his system but addicting to him. Though he never thought about it, war had shaped Jovan into the person he was tonight.

Tonight, Jovan had not gone home. He had stumbled into town

and started walking. He had begun drinking, and now in his drunken stupor, he was having a hard time escaping the personal Hell that were his thoughts.

Jovan knew he could blame only himself for the brutal fighting. Ultimately, when he saw the crimson red he would bleed each time he was hurt, he was looking at the real reason he was here. It was all because of his bloodline. He would share the same legacy his great grandfather, grandfather, and father all shared.

He was a knight.

Jovan had sparkling, shining, sterling, armor, and a beautiful white horse, a picture of nobility in living color. It was so real to be clad in metal and riding high into battle. Nothing could make his hands sweat and muscles tense, his heart race and his adrenaline trigger, like running into battle.

But Jovan knew, his heart had been tainted. He was a person who could love with so much passion. A warrior had no use for empathy, and was always in fight mode, and this was why he sometimes felt like he had lost himself.

Suddenly, something cold and familiar began to fall from the sky. Jovan looked up as it fell to replenish the tortured earth. Hello, rain; hello, old friend.

The rain began to fall into his dirty blonde hair, washing down his entire body. It permeated his thin clothes like a thousand needles and he began to shiver.

It was then that he felt so alive.

Jovan had been holding a bottle of brandy. It had brought him to a drunken state, his emerald eyes now bloodshot. The sky had started to become lighter; Jovan knew he should be headed home. He had been in his town square taking refuge under an old oak tree during the rain. As he looked around, he noticed birds flying in and landing in the tree. They would soon sing their morning songs and the town would be awakened, and in a few mere hours it would be bustling with all the townspeople and merchants.

Jovan turned to face the sunrise and tried to figure out what he should do. He needed to go home now, so that no one would see him like this. Jovan was a hero, he was a legend, he was of another world, and he knew he could not let a drunken night out tarnish his storybook image. Jovan could see his town's colors reflected in the sky as gold and crimson rays burst through the night to bring in a new day.

Jovan tiredly began to drag himself home, following the straight path he knew, and headed to his house at the edge of the forest. He loved his secluded house; his tortured mind and body needed time for rest and serenity, and this was the only place he would ever find it.

"Jovan!" he heard behind him, and two running feet trying to catch up. Jovan stopped. "Jovan! Wait, Jovan!" Jovan sighed and internally groaned- he knew who the voice belonged to. It was Torin, his adolescent squire. Torin was sixteen, and he looked up to Jovan so much, because soon he would be a knight himself, and he hoped to be one of Jovan's status.

"Torin," Jovan began, "Go get some rest. You should not be up this early." Torin glared at him. "You should not be out this late," he said, then realized he had no place to speak to his teacher this way. "What I do is none of your business. I am just here to teach you things. You listen to what I have to say and make of it what you will. Anything else?"

Torin cast his gaze down at the cobblestone street, as he was ashamed of how he had acted. "I just need to know if you are coming to the banquet tonight. I was on the way to your house but found you here instead. The king sent me to find out. He needs to know if all of you are coming."

Jovan's heart started racing. The banquet. He completely forgot- it was a parade of laughter, music, booze, and nobles showing of their nobility. Because they had achieved a victory, the king was to host a banquet in honor of the Hawthorne knights. But Jovan, though he was part of it often, hated the pageantry and the honor; after killing men, he never wanted to celebrate.

"Yes, I'll be there." It wasn't really a question; being at the banquet was expected of him. He had been a big part of their victory, leading his soldiers to the final, brutal attack; and he was a legend in his kingdom. The king, he knew, respected him; and he must go. To be noble in the midst of oppression was a wild fantasy that he lived every day.

Jovan turned to leave and Torin whimpered behind him. "I'll see you tonight, then," Jovan said, letting him know that he must be going home now. Torin had the spirit of a knight. It was all he wanted in this world. But Jovan knew he did not have the heart. It took a special soul for knighthood. Torin would know the skills and he would have the drive to fight for his town. But he would not be able to mentally handle the pain, the emotional torture, the brutality of some men, and the way some nights led you to your darkest places.

The sleep Jovan had that day was an escape, a lapse in time that separated him from all the other things. He knew that only a few hours separated him from being in a room with beautiful people, beautiful and timeless things; beautiful words and feelings, dancing, drinking, and honor.

His knights, just like any other time, would be there beside him. Their faces would give him hope. He had seen them all in the middle of hell, and they had come back from it, and they were strong enough to laugh again.

When Jovan awakened, rays of sunset cast through his window. The atmosphere woke him. Jovan knew it was time to go.

He sat and pondered things for a minute. He was a bit hung over, his breath reeked of alcohol and tobacco. His silk shirt waited for him in his closet. He went to adorn the garment and comb his tangled and dirty hair. His beautiful face smiled back in the mirror at him, because he could not help but feel a bit of pride as he thought about the evening to come.

Jovan stood at the castle doors. The castle took his breath away every time he saw it, though he saw it often. It was a symbol of strength in their town. It was beautiful, it was gigantic; it was majestic and glorious. It humbled him with so much emotion, it made him feel so small. To be a part of this was something from a dream. And he lived it each day.

Jovan stepped inside and was immediately hit with scents,

commotion, and lights throughout the ballroom. The party was already in full swing. Bread and fruit was on the table and so many people crowded the room. As he walked in, everyone stopped and stared. "Jovan!" a group of women stood near the door, gossiping and laughing with one another. "So glad you made it!" A woman in green, with dark hair and a kind face, had stepped forward to greet him. "Thank you, my lady," Jovan responded. He smiled gently and scanned the room for his brothers in arms.

He spotted them over in the corner, a large rectangular table was lined with his men. So many brawny soldiers were talking and laughing amongst themselves. They were a rowdy bunch drinking gallons of whiskey and chanting, yelling at the top of their lungs. Jovan blushed slightly at the noise they were making. When they spotted him, they began to shout his name and usher him over. Jovan made his way over to the table.

As soon as he approached them, one person stood out to him. It was his fellow knight and eternal enemy- Samuel. Samuel had always been cold toward Jovan; they had fought together with a tense rivalry. Their blood ran hot and angry when they fought side-by-side. Samuel was a dark shadow in the room full of colors and life. His grey eyes peered up at him, his face darkened with black hair and a menacing grin.

But tonight, Samuel was not alone; he was with a girl.

When God had made her, he had used blue from the purest sapphire. Her skin was porcelain and blushed, and perfectly flawless and beautiful. Her hair was honey golden succulence that dripped from her shoulders down to her breasts.

Jovan had loved many girls, and many times he had not woken up alone. He would always wake up the next morning unable to shake off the regret. He would have the girls in a very personal way, and they would be heartbroken as he rolled over from them the next day, with no passion in his eyes.

Letting them go would always be hard, but he would always know that it was bound to happen. Because when Jovan loved them, they gave their all to him. They were drawn in, they became hooked.

But when he would bid them goodbye they, too, would know it was over, and always picture him as theirs, and dream of him each night, but never hold him again.

He wondered what her name was, what her hand would feel like in his; he wondered what her voice would sound like with his name on her pretty lips.

He wanted nothing more than to have her beside him, to feel her heartbeat, to feel her touch lingering on his skin. Of all the girls he had ever seen, she was the most perfect.

Jovan knew that when he would leave here, he would be high from living, he would have sort of an immortal feeling, he would feel strong again, he would feel disassociated from the prison that was his own mind. He would go home and all fears be lost. All questions he ever had, all sadness and worry, would be gone, because he had just been celebrated and he had just won a victory. This was part of what kept him going, the applause from people, the parties and the praise, the way they saw him for all his strengths instead of how he really felt-weak and trapped in this world of being a soldier.

"Jovan," he heard a voice over all the white noise in his mind, "Jovan, they are about to recognize us!" it was Henry, one of his colleagues, sitting near him and had apparently noticed that Jovan was mentally wandering. "Henry, you know I don't care for these things," Jovan stated. Henry laughed at Jovan. A deep, hearty, lively laugh-a laugh that would make anyone nearby look over to see what the commotion was about. "you know, they have parties for us, celebrate us, then send us out to get killed," Jovan added. Henry slapped Jovan on the back. His hand was large and bony, with so much strength inside it. But Jovan did not flinch. He flashed a smile up at Henry, Who was standing beside him, holding a mug of beer, the beer slowly dripping on the floor because Henry was tilting it to the side a little too much.

Hawthorne was prideful. They would never give up fighting as long as their soldiers could fight. They were known to other towns as the one not to mess with, the ones that had an unspeakable wrath.

Jovan was proud to be a part of it but all too often, the weight of it all was carried on his shoulders.

A jester for the king shoved his way through the crowd of people and made it up to a large table in the middle, where guests of nobility sat. Normally, he would never get away with something like this. The man, dressed in red and green silk pants and shirt, grabbed the edge of the large wooden table and hoisted his way up to stand on it, careful not to knock over food or drinks. "Ladies and Gentlemen, Royalty and those in the court, We all know the reason we are here tonight enjoying this wonderful feast!" he began announcing. For the first time tonight, the room went silent. The jester's voice rang out over the whole crowd.

The palace was usually a very quiet place, business took place here, and important guests were in and out, always presenting themselves with dignity. But tonight, no man would say anything about tonight being inappropriate or loud, because though rich men loved being proper, rich men also loved to drink, and would never miss an opportunity to do so.

"We are here because these men, here in the corner, these men, have achieved a great victory against our neighboring town and ending a feud that has lasted over one hundred years. This is truly a cause for celebration. Their bravery and skill is rare, and of a rare breed. Ladies and Gentlemen, the knights of Hawthorne."

In a loud and chilling unanimous cheer, the entire room came to life. There was yelling and whistling and clapping. Jovan stood, along with his comrades, but this should have brought him to his knees- this was such a thing of honor, such a thing of blessing. He was among one of the most admired in his entire town. Jovan was numb over his entire body. His heartbeat seemed to be the only thing he could feel and the room was so silent it seemed he would have been able to hear as it pumped his noble blood throughout his body. He felt that it was hard to breathe, he felt that there was not enough space in his heart to accept such appreciation. He felt that it was so hard to stand. Jovan was humbled. Men of a certain kind, men of certain blood, men of certain dignity became knights. Jovan had always knew, ever since he was young, that this is what his future would be. He knew he would be faced with the fighting and the war, and so much love at the same time. He knew he would ride a horse and swing a mace, and use a sword, but he never knew his heart would break so much or that the dreams would keep him up at night. He never knew he would get so much love for the hardest things he had ever had to do.

At this time, the palace was filled with drunken nobility, and music crept into the atmosphere. One by one the people began to dance and before he knew it, almost everyone had gotten up from their food and were mingling and dancing together.

Jovan was quite shy in certain situations. He was not the type to start dancing in front of everyone else. Now, however, many people were making their way over to the ball room floor, and the band had started to play jolly dancing music. Some girls standing in the corner stared at Jovan and began waving at him. When he returned the wave, they giggled and laughed with one another. He stood out in any crowd with his good looks; female attention was another thing he had to be accustomed to.

Samuel and his date sat wide-eyed a few seats down from Jovan, as they had not yet joined the rest of the crowd. Samuel had his arm around her and she leaned in, facing him. A candle from the table created a shadow around them, creating a shroud for the two of them to be lost in while the rest of the world went about their insanity. They seemed very inapproachable; perhaps that was why no one was asking them to come dance or have some drinks. Jovan, on the other hand, had drank his fill and was trying to spare himself the embarassment of dancing under the influence. He rubbed his eyes. His vision was beginning to become blurry, his head was beginning to spin.

After drinking the night before, and drinking now yet again, Jovan's thoughts were hazy and his balance was hard to control. He was focused on being able to sit upright in his chair. He sat on the same side of the table as Samuel and his lady friend. Out of the corner of his eye, he glanced at her, studying her moves, and trying to get the courage to talk to her.

It was like he had seen her before, like she was from a dream he had had long ago. She was one of the beautiful girls, he had thought- the kind that only dated men like knights. They were untouchable, they were unreal. They were a class all on their own. They were the only thing that made Jovan stop and catch his breath and take a second look as they passed.

These were the type of women that Jovan would always stop to admire for just a second. Sometimes, he had to apologize for staring. They were so superior to him, he imagined; a dirty drinking soldier was nothing compared to their flawless skin, their angelic laughs, their sunshine smiles. They were out there, but he seldom saw them in his town.

Through his hazy and obscure line of sight, Jovan spotted a figure coming his way. An hourglass figure, clad in a black and flowing dress. The dress floated toward him as she came near. There was an elegance about it, real and classy, like the fabric itself had been cut out from the night sky. The wearer, however, was innocent and fumbling, a young girl of debutante age that was trying to fool all the men around her. But she could not fool Jovan, Because he knew. The girl in the dress was a daughter of a noble merchant in his town, wealthy from his business of ginseng and imported teas. And just like every other man around here, upon having a daughter, he would be arranging a marriage for her soon; But she, being a romantic, was determined to find true love, and here she was doing her best to do just that.

Her name was River. She was seventeen, and almost beautiful, but she did not carry herself in a way that was flattering and she was so obviously putting forth extra effort to seem cultured and mature, she was always staring and talking, saying way too much for a girl of her time. She had skin like ivory and auburn hair, red with tints of brown and when she touched Jovan, it burned into him like smoldering ash. He snapped out of his daze and met her eyes, also like fire, because they were sparked with amber, and she looked at him with a sweltering passion, with hunger and longing like never before.

"I owe you a congratulations on your victory, Sire Jovan," she started. She reached out her hand and Jovan took it. She bowed to him. "Thank you, River," He replied, "It was not just me. It was all of these men. I could not have done this on my own." River smiled at him. She did enjoy this attention. "I know it is unlady like, but I was wondering, if you would like to dance." Jovan stared. He did not want to dance with her, he did not want to fuel the inferno, however he felt her ardent presence and her breath was like whiskey, searing into his throat when he breathed it in.

"Yes, River, I would like to," he replied, hesitating. River grabbed his hand and led him to dance. Jovan was trying to focus on keeping his balance, he knew he would face the crowd and he would have to socialize with all the nobility in his town. So he began to mentally prepare himself.

So many people gasped at him, they would turn and whisper to one another when he would walk by. They saw him as a surreal figure that had immense power. He was just a man, which is what many failed to see.

River held onto Jovan, she took refuge in his strong hold and his towering height. She knew all the dances and she was good company. During their time at the ball, Jovan was approached by many people. They all believed in him, they said, and they all knew he was the strongest, the stealthiest, the most legendary. Jovan was a legend in his town, in fact, they all knew he fought his battles with passion and without fear and he would never back down from any opponent.

Jovan was known from towns over. Jovan had never been defeated. Jovan was known for his presence, For riding out in the battlefield without flinching, for his gallant white horse, for all the times he came home with blood on his iron clad body. He was known for fighting off dozens of men at a time and for unmatched skill and stealth. Jovan was his father's son, he was the product of bloodlines pure and rich, bred to perfection to produce a fighter like him. He was honored and praised. He was one of the chosen in his town and he believed that knowing this kept him going through many of his hardest days.

River held to Jovan, she soaked up every ounce of his attention. Jovan humored her. He kept his hand in the small of her back, he led her around the ball room and the people greeted the two of them as they paraded around in their extravagant display of wealth, from their clothes to the sophistication they carried themselves with. River was an Angel that had fallen from grace. She was a nice girl, she had a good upbringing, but she was rather fille de joie at times and she had tainted her own reputation as the innocent daughter of a noble man.

She kept trying to pull him in with her seductive gaze, her flawless figure floating over the dance floor, her black dress clung to her but fanned out to cover the ballroom floor. It glided with her, following her flawless movements, and her feminine frame was tightly pressed to him as she reveled in his presence, as fueling her desires seem to make her thirst even more. He avoided looking into her eyes as he knew he would be under her spell. She was a

Jovan had had many nights where he was not alone. He would get a woman into his bed and into his home and he would spend the night with her, and they would drink and talk, and he would always tell himself that he could forgive himself later, because he knew that there was never love between the two of them. With every girl he ever had, he would hold her and keep her close but he knew his heart was empty and his hunger would persist. Jovan knew he no longer wanted a lady of the night.

And there were a lot of girls. They were always approaching Jovan and always beckoning him in. All of them wanted to be with someone like him and get to be invited to his bed. It was sinful and it was dark, but they pushed these thoughts out of their minds when they reminded themselves of who he was.

To be with a legend was like a dance in a dream- the haziness, the power, the strong grip that made them melt in his hands. The fine line between reality and floating on clouds was indistinguishable. To be touched by him, to be held by him, to be loved by him was incredible.

As Jovan went into his third dance with River, He spotted her. He spotted Gracie across the room, as she stood against the palace wall like an ornament, like a fixture for the party. Samuel was nowhere in his line of sight. Jovan excused himself from River as she held to him with a vice grip, but finally letting go when she knew she could not hold him back.

Jovan did not know what was happening. Jovan did not know what was drawing him over, he did not know what he would say or what to do, he just knew he had to hear her voice. He imagined it was like an eruption to knock him out of his monotonous reality, and her laugh would be confetti raining down on him afterward. He wanted to feel her hair against his cheek and he wanted to know her life, to know everything about her. She was much like a fictional being, like something he would have never dreamed existed, and something he could have never even fathomed in the darkest corners of his mind.

As he walked over, her gaze followed him, and as he got closer, she began to smile. Her smile was the sun as it warmed up the room around him and beckoned him to get closer. He felt hypnotized as she lured him in.

"Jovan, of Hawthorne," She stated. Jovan returned her smile. "You-you know my name?" He wondered, taken aback. When she looked at him she looked further than just his eyes, she peered deep into his being. "Sire, everyone knows you. Don't try to humble yourself, you know this is true. And everyone knows what a warrior you are." Jovan began to utter a response. She was truly sophisticated and truly refined and she showed confidence as well as humility. Jovan had shut out all the commotion around him, her beauty was deafening.

"My lady," he began, "I do not take credit for my victories, I work with all my men to earn it, and we do not accept thanks for doing our service." She gave him a flirty look, one that said his reasoning was not credible, like she had heard it all before. "And you, are quite known yourself," he stated, "would you like to dance?" He extended his hand like an offering, and she took it as they went to the middle of the ball room.

Jovan left River standing alone, arms crossed in the middle of the ballroom. Her mouth fell open, and a look of shock filled her expression. She looked defeated, and sadly walked over to take a seat nearby the knight's table.

Jovan could not believe that she was right here so close to him. She was his drug, she was his ecstasy. The two of them were toxic but the feeling was so numbing and nothing else in the world would matter. The menagerie of people around ceased to exist. He did not care what any of them had to say. Jovan had never felt this way around another person before. He felt much lighter on his feet, he felt as if any move he made would be amplified a thousand times. He felt stronger and renewed. He felt his heart beats banging into him, hitting him each time like an anvil. Though being with her was so easy, it was difficult at the same time. He knew she was another man's, and the hands that held her now would be replaced by the ones of his enemy just a short time from now. Those hands were a little darker, a little more sinister, and Jovan only hoped they would hold her in the way they should.

"Jovan," she started, laughing a little. "you are not much for words, are you?" Jovan laughed back with her. "I don't know where to start," he replied, this was so true. He wanted to ask her everything but he felt lost, he had no idea where to begin. She made him stop and think.

Maybe, he thought, he should try and talk more; he worried she would see him as dull; he worried she would not feel the chemistry he felt with her.

He knew he would have to stop if he did not want to get addicted, But Gracie was so full of life and so hypnotic, and he saw time melting away as he spent it with her, and if they were to spend a lifetime together, the days would blend into months and months would fade into years, and it would all end in a blurry and blissful oblivion, and he would have no regrets.

"Would you start by telling me why you and Samuel do not like one another, all the other knights seem to get along with you both so well." Jovan froze completely, he was at a loss for words. He never seemed to understand what had happened between the both of them to cause such a fight. He had fought beside Samuel many times and he had even shielded him and killed for him. But outside of the battlefield, there was a tension that neither of them could overcome.

"We have a rivalry," Jovan began, "that goes back for years. When we were jousting or riding through the forest, or talking to the king, it seemed to always be a competition, and ever since we were young we were trying to outdo one another." Gracie paused for a minute, processing this, and met Jovan's gaze again. He could feel his hands begin to sweat, he could feel the color flushing from his body. Maybe he had said too much.

Jovan and Samuel were always in a race, always trying to be better than the other. Jovan wanted to be more admired, more adorned with trophies; he wanted roses thrown at him after he won a tournament, and he wanted his name shouted after every battle won. Samuel wanted the same, and had the same drive as Jovan to earn it all. They were so alike in so many ways, they both fought gallantly and fearlessly beside on another for a common cause.

"You seem like a good man," she replied, "and you seem to be a better warrior." As there was a pause in the music, there was a lull in the crowd, and Jovan realized it was getting late, the party was beginning to die. "Hey," he breathed, "follow me."

Jovan grabbed Gracie and took off, like children running to hide from scolding parents. "I want you to see this place, it is beautiful up here," he explained, as they headed away from the ball room and down a castle corridor, Jovan holding her by the hand and half-running the whole way there. They found themselves outside in the courtyard.

Out here, there was a stone gazebo and walkway. And overflowing onto the walking paths and up into the palace walls were tons of exotic plants and flowers from all over the world. This, Jovan had heard, was the only place where these plants could be found here in Hawthorne. And if one sat in the gazebo, stars would peek through the intricate stonework at the top, creating a blanket of solace that could only be found on a summer night like this.

This summer had been sweltering. The air was heavy, and constricting, and thick like vapor. The flowers produced an amorous fragrance that was covering the atmosphere like a thin silky robe. God had painted the night sky a nice shade of charcoal black and had cut out diamonds to scatter across the sky. A silver moon was bright enough to illuminate the area around them.

It was one of the castle's hidden secrets; winding hallways, doorways, rooms and hideaways-it was magical and beautiful just like this night had been.

It was his favorite place in the world to be. He could come here and see the lovely picture that mother nature had painted. He could exist amongst it all, as it was so surreal. Petals covered the stone walkway through the path. Candles lit the way for them as they lined the walkway and the gazebo. It was his Eden- nothing could go wrong here.

Gracie was delighted. "Oh, this place is so beautiful! I've never seen some of these plants before." They strolled around the courtyard along the paved and rocky path. Jovan had come here often, upon visiting the castle, and had seen it during the day many times, but he knew it looked much more beautiful at night. Just as they had walked into the gazebo, a gruff voice cut into their isolated world.

When they were in the gazebo, small patches of light shone through the slats on the roof, cast from the moon and the stars above them.

"Gracie, where have you been?" Samuel stomped out to the courtyard. His presence was so dark. He was so cold and edgy, his voice cut into the darkness like a sharpened sword. "I have been looking for you half the night! We need to go." Jovan must have been hidden in the shadows, because upon spotting his promised in the gazebo, Samuel did not see his enemy. As Samuel got closer, he saw the masculine outline and Jovan turned, allowing them to face one another.

"Oh, it's you," he scoffed. He came closer and grabbed Gracie by the arm, jerking her away from him. "I trust you have taken care of her," he added. Jovan was silent, not sure if he should be ashamed or glad for the few minutes they had together. Jovan, still silent, turned to walk away and back inside. As he approached Samuel, he vaguely stopped to tell him, "of course. She is all yours." And then he forced himself to go.

As Jovan walked back down into the ball room, he was riddled with thoughts. Maybe he should have never spoken to her. But he could never have gone on knowing that he never even tried. Because now that he knew her name, now that he knew her touch, he felt more complete than he had in a long time. He felt life was renewed inside of him.

Now, it was late. The gargantuan clock that hung on the ballroom wall told him that is was after midnight. He had been drinking, dancing, and socializing the entire evening and now, he was exhausted. Dirty glasses littered the tables of the ballroom which had been decorated so immaculately, but was now ruined by food and dishes everywhere, alcohol spills on the floor, and tobacco smoke creating a ubiquitous fog throughout the atmosphere.

As he tried to enter back into the ball room, trying to go unnoticed, a desperate River came running up to him. She immediately grabbed him. "Jovan! There you are, everyone is leaving." Her voice was whiny and high pitched and her tone was desperate. "Jovan, let me leave with you," She begged. She gazed up at him with a lusty look in her eye and her touch was sparking with flame as she put her hands on his waist.

A covet in her aura, an ardor for his company, he knew he could never fuel the fire. "I'm sorry, River," he refused, "I would rather be alone tonight." River's eyes were pleading, her voice wavering and shallow like her namesake. "Jovan, will I see you again?" Jovan grabbed her, hugged her, and began to turn away. "You will, River. Thank you tonight for your company."

To love Jovan was an honor, a privilege to know him in his most intimate state. But for Jovan to love was hard for him, he found it hard to channel so much emotion into a single person and to trust another with those feelings. When it came to opening up, Jovan was a weighted door with an abyss of darkness behind it.

Jovan's mind was filled with a hundred racing thoughts, a million what-ifs. He was confused, he was honored for killing others from another town, and he was let down because his enemy would always have what he wished he could have. He was loved so much by every person in his town, yet he felt such resentment for himself. After all the alcohol and all the music, all the colors and all the honor, all he could do for himself now is go home and hopefully lose himself in sleep.

Jovan did sleep that night. He was lost in the void of his mind and he was at peace for once. He could escape his reality, he could be numb to the world. As much as he felt, it was also easy to numb himself. He had looked death in the face and he had seen it happen in so many different ways. Men with their faces covered with metal, to make death seem as if it had no face. And also to make fear have no face. Fear was like satan, it would find itself in the most intimate corners of his thoughts and his life, and then creep up and show itself, but he never turned away from it. The sound of victory yells far overshadowed the feeling of fear.

Chapter 2

Incandescent beams of light shone through Jovan's window the next morning. It was a brand new day, it was a brand new chance. However, not even the sun's glory could get him up this morning. Jovan ached in every joint and every muscle. His Emerald eyes were still not seeing very clear. His head was pounding from the inside.

Jovan was a Michealangelo's David. He was rock solid. He was cold and tough like marble on his exterior. But he was crafted so elegantly, His muscles chiseled out from the finest flesh and his stature tall and strong. Jovan's strength was at the highest caliber of any. His eyes were emerald stone, and his hair was a dirty blonde that, when hit by the sun, would reflect its golden rays and gave his silhouette an angelic feel. When he was hit by a weapon, a sword, mace, or arrow, he would rely on a layer of metal to protect it all and keep him from death. Flying through a battle on a horse was like flying close to God as death was a shadow around him.

When Jovan fought, he always knew what could happen to him. Men were killed all the time in battle. But, for some reason, he was always spared. He always made it home, and he knew each time that he was lucky- because so easily, it could have been him.

Today Jovan moaned as he felt the aching and he knew that he may have survived the party the night before, but today he would pay. Everything in his mortal being was stiff. The previous night seemed like a hazy memory to him. He knew he had danced and celebrated, but the part he remembered the most was the time he had spent with a divine being, the star in his otherwise void galaxy.

About this time, Jovan was startled by a loud knocking. There was someone at the door. "Jovan, Jovan you have to open the door! I hope you are in there!" Jovan knew that voice, it was Torin, and he breathed out a breath of annoyance as he got up to open the door. Torin stood plastered against the doorframe, obviously anxious. "Sire, you are needed," he began, "I was sent to tell you...You have to meet the other men in the town square. There is word about a sniper in the forest, waiting to kill off our people. You have to go find him." Jovan knew that within a few minutes, he would be at it again, and for all he knew, he may not come home.

"Torin, who told you about this?" He asked, as Torin appeared anxious. "It's the king," he began, "the king was spreading the word, all the other knights already knew. You were the last to find out. You have to go now." Jovan paused for a minute. Torin was hard to deal with sometimes. "Why was I the last to find out?" Torin shrugged. "Your house is the furthest away, Sire." Torin choked, nervous to speak to his superior. Jovan swallowed his pride and his frustration. He slapped Torin on the shoulder. "Ok, Let's go," Jovan breathed. And just like that, He prepared for battle.

Right now, he was still half asleep and sloppily hung over. He could not share Torin's panic like he should. The alcohol had drowned it out and made him mellow and he could not see the point in being in a hurry.

Hastily and flawlessly, Jovan put on his armor. Each piece was designed for him specially. After his whole body was covered, he was an iron warrior. His sterling, glittering ensemble would be seen by the townspeople and everyone would part, letting him through, and they would see Jovan's coat of arms and cheer. Going from man to warrior in a few minutes was one of his greatest talents.

Jovan's horse was larger than life just like him. The image was from a story book, about a land far away where the animals and people were pure and peaceful. It was an image of pure white with a mane of ashes, smoldering down past the side of his neck. Then the beast, though large and strong, would so limberly gallop away into a blurred image of grace.

Torin assisted Jovan as he put on the armor, piece by piece, and assisted him to get the horse saddled and ready. Jovan would hand Torin his weapons, and he would find his way into the saddle, a familiar place to him. When Jovan was on his horse he felt he was on top of the world and an unfathomable sense of power. He knew now, just like so many other times before, there was no looking back.

Jovan had a mace and a bow with arrows, and he also had with him a sword. The sword was for desperate measures, he would hope to use one of the others before resorting to it. But Jovan was skilled with a sword and his aim was flawless, so no matter which one Jovan chose to turn to, he hoped it would be enough to make the shot he needed. And Jovan knew with a sniper hiding out, he would also need to be on high alert-arrows and traps coming out of every direction, so he knew he would also have to rely on his mind and hope that he could outsmart the one hiding in the bushes.

When Jovan got to town a league of men were gathered, waiting for direction from the king. They all sat ready to go on horseback. Townspeople were hovering around in the background, hoping to overhear the business of the court. Jovan spotted a hazel stallion clad in familiar armor. The rider was complete with his helmet, but Jovan could see right through and he knew he was looking into the face of his rival. They would be fighting side by side, they would kill for one another and they would ride together, but they would never seek an understanding. All the drama and all the rivalry would be put aside for battle, but would never permanently go away.

Samuel was a darkened soul. He was a kindred spirit; Jovan knew they were so much the same, but Samuel had been damaged and ruined by the tragedies of war. It had made him a bitter man. The experiences of war would forever taint his heart and damage his soul. He was not a friend at all to Jovan. They had never seen eye to eye- it was a rivalry, Jovan figured.

"Warriors," A jester had found his way to the middle of their colorful crowd. He was the messenger for the King. "There is word of a sniper hiding out in the forest," he began, his voice booming and much more deep than one would have expected it to be. "The task the King has for you is to go into the forest, find him, and bring him back to the palace to let the King decide his punishment. You men must not return until he is found; word is that Januvia is not ready to give up their fight, and they have sent one of their best archers. Godspeed, Noble men."

Samuel and his large dark steed were stirring around in the edge of the crowd, the horse restlessly moving from side to side, as Samuel put his focus on trying to control it. When the Jester had finished his words, Samuel set his horse into full speed and yelled, "We go onward!" and the others followed closely behind him. They must have looked so brave and gallant, they must have seemed so fearless and eager. Jovan had to slow his horse to keep from getting ahead. With his delay, he would be at the back of the division. He could spot Samuel way ahead. He was a dark rider; He was like a shadow that would creep up upon his enemy and take them to a dark place they would never escape from.

The wind on Jovan's face was chilling though it was the middle of summer. Dew still clung to the grass this morning. Jovan took a deep breath in. His lungs were brand new and full of life and they kept carrying him onward. His mind was clear today and he felt capable. If only certain things would not get in his way.

This mission was about riding into the forest and claiming back their town. For now, this was, ongoing. The battle that they had fought so hard to win had so obviously not been the thing that would end it. Januvia was not going to give up. Their stubbornness and their brutality were as old as time and the feud they had with Hawthorne was fueled by years of rivalry. The fight had started one hundred years ago exactly. Januvia and Hawthorne had been the same town at one time. They lived and worked together, they were neighbors and merchants living in peace. The knights fought with one another and the troop was twice as large. They were a force to be reckoned with. When the prince was born, he was surprisingly born with a twin brother.

The two brothers fought their entire lives. From childhood, they fought as each wanted to prove that they were superior and would one day earn the title of king. In the back of his mind Prince Favian knew that his brother, Prince Merek, had been born first, therefore making him the oldest, and the title would most likely go to him. Favian was bitter at this. His whole life's work and purpose would go to waste if Merek earned the throne.

So, when the twins reached adulthood, Favian declared a fight with Merek and a battle ensued. The battle lasted for an entire week. Men had been ripped apart and killed and wounded so badly that they could no longer be identified. The actual battle, much like the battle in their lives, never ended. Upon never reaching an understanding, the town was split in half and Hawthorne was named after Favian's first born and Januvia after Merek's.

The two men ruled mercilessly after that with infinite power now in the hands of them both. It was a tyranny, they were bitter and brutal. Both had gotten what they wanted but they each had so much guilt for treating the other the way they did. Perhaps, everyone wondered, that was why they were both so mean.

But that was years ago. As time passed, the feud still reigned, but the fight between kings was over. There was no real reason to keep fighting except for the sheer joy of victory and to know that, even after all this time, victory could be won and hopefully all the blood shed could be put to rest.

Favian and Merek faced the same thing as Jovan faced. Because of his blood lines, because of his nobility, he was put into a world of war. War would surely bring about peace, he always reasoned, but the peace never seemed to last for long. He knew, because of who he was, he would live this life forever and it would become who he was. And because of who he was, he now longed for victory, he longed for stamina to fight every endless battle.

How much could his heart go on? How long could his simple flesh last, it was only protected by a layer of metal. Could the cross on his shield deflect any arrows, could the resilience in his mind keep him going? Because either way, Jovan knew, the fight would not wait for him-it would go on and it would rage as long as it needed to take men's lives and to destroy towns, to ravage crops and livestock and then somehow end in a beautiful victory.

As the influx of soldiers galloped from town, Jovan stayed toward the back of the group. He would be the last to enter the forest. But he was not afraid; he could protect himself if need be and if chaos ensued, it would be in God's hands. He could see them up ahead. They were a barricade of iron men with nothing to do but prove themselves. His age of warfare was dangerous for those with a mortal mindset.

As Jovan had gotten out of the town he could see a full view of the woodland behind him that he was about to enter. There was a trail in the forest that led to Januvia. Most people of Hawthorne had no business there, but the trail also cutaway into several different paths that led to a few other towns and even one that led to the docks, where larger than life merchant ships would come and go, bringing prosperity to all that endeavored in that line of work.

Jovan's aquamarine eyes spotted something up above that was changing the sky-the sky, once oppressive and cloudless, was peppered with arrows. Jovan had not yet entered the forest. He knew that those who had were right in the middle of it. He could have turned his horse the other way to hide out until it was all over and then ride back to safety. But Jovan had an innate sense in his being, of valor and virtue, and he knew he could never turn away and turn his back on his people. Jovan gritted his teeth and commanded his horse to go onward.

There was obviously more than one sniper, he had figured out, but that was the frightening part-he did not know how many men and how many arrows he might face. Januvia had used this tactic well, playing mind games with their opponents. They were hoping to overwhelm them, catch them off guard, and use the art of panic to bring them down. There were already familiar sounds coming from the trees- shouting, yelling, baying of horses and metal clashing together as it hit. It was emphatic and resonated off everything around him. He entered the forest threshold expecting any and every thing to be used against him in a foggy collision of both worlds.

There were so many men- Januvia soldiers were scattered all along the forest and were fighting his companions in the dense trees and grasses. The dirt was now stained crimson and the path no longer mattered, because every corner and every thicket had a knight waiting on his next move. Jovan had fought in the castle, a barrier of solid rock to separate him and the enemy. He had fought in the open battlefield where the space allowed room to see his comrades and come to their aide if need be. This, he thought, was far different than any other war he had been in.

With a solid and empty clank from his armor, he knew he had been hit from behind.

Jovan turned to face a man standing horseless but armed with a sword. He swung at Jovan as Jovan grabbed his sword and brought it down on him. Being on horseback, Jovan could bring the sword to this guy's throat and easily get through the gap between his helmet and chest piece. Jovan attempted this move as the knight quickly grabbed Jovan's sword and took it from his hand. Jovan turned his horse to the side so the sword would not go into them. He got out his mace and swung it like a pendulum into the man's armoured skull. He crashed to the ground and lay there helpless. Jovan bent to retrieve his sword and moved along to face another offender. This time, the guy was riding high on an elegant copper stallion and came charging at him full force. His mace was swinging with power as it bluntly crashed into Jovan's side. He wavered a bit, his ribcage numb and his right lung gasping for air, but Jovan stayed on his horse and he somewhere deep inside of him found his fighting instinct.

This, Jovan knew, was part of being a born soldier. From his lineage of knighthood, it had been perfected over the years. His brawn and his stamina was a big part of it, yes-but the main part was using your head, knowing which moves to make, because In battle every second counted and your fate could rely on which move you made next. With one wrong move, he could end up on the ground and be twice as vulnerable. Without his instinct, he would never know how to move as fast as he needed. His beautiful face, mind, and body worked as one to take down anyone who tried to destroy it.

Maybe, he thought, maybe that was why he was so reveled. He had amazing skill and technique that could not be learned-it was innate. The people knew what a treasure he was, an honorable man that would do his town good.

And here he found himself again in the face of a rival. Jovan still had his mace out and he rode toward the man and took a swing. He was shaken but did not fall from his horse. The caliber of their fighting skills were both insurmountable. A feeling of anger surged throughout Jovan instantaneously at that moment. He would not let a faceless enemy wish death upon him.

Jovan, with his bare fists, began to fight the man. They punched one another and Jovan grabbed his sides as he ducked, hoping to unsteady him from his horse. The man came at him with another blow with an armored fist and just then, Jovan grabbed him by the arm and held it, so that he could not escape the hold. Jovan tilted him back in the saddle and, grabbing his sword with the other hand, made a clean cut into his abdomen. Adrenaline replaced the blood in his body. Jovan continued to fight and show no mercy. He would fight until his death; because the honor he would have was worth so much more than living a life that was empty.

So the fight went on like this for the entire day and up into the night. By this point he was halfway into the woods as he had went wherever the fight had led him. He felt no hunger or longing for rest, as there was a job to do, and he worked with integrity. Some of the soldiers began to get weak. Their energy was waning and their hope wearing down. Still, they all pushed forward and kept fighting. The king was expecting a single archer to be brought back to him. What he got instead was a blood bath of combat.

During battle, time went away; thoughts went away, daily life ceased from existing. Wartime was the only thing that mattered at that moment. Those that persisted were those that survived and there was time for rest later.

Jovan could feel the energy of the chaos slowly fading. He knew that he had almost made it. He hoped that maybe one day, what he was fighting for would stand for something. Maybe he would go down in history or maybe he would alter the world. As long as this would mean something, he felt that was enough to fight for.

The men in his group were beginning to aggregate. They had found one another. He would not know who had perished. It would soon be time to leave and the ones that did not return would be the ones that would be left behind, because there was no way to tell if they had made it. As Jovan stayed with his group, he saw two others approach.

The two men were his fellow knights- Sire Anaxis and Sire Benedict. There horses trotted in sync with one another. The moon shone off of their armor to make them appear glowing, like torches in an ugly place. As they got closer, Jovan could see Anaxis had a body with him on the back of his horse. The body was still clad in battle gear but the helmet was gone. Looking into the face of the deceased, he could see his friend Henry.

Jovan felt a shot of pain go throughout his body. He thought of Henry from the party the night before. He had been so jovial that night. His spirit was unbreakable. He was always the cheerful one and the one that you could count on for anything. Henry was one of the older knights, he had taught Jovan so much in his time. A man with such skill and strength could not have been brought down easily. Jovan began to feel a cold sweat in his hands as he held his horse's reins. What he felt was sadness and anger. The battle may have been won, but the loss would never be made up for.

"We found him leaned against one of the trees," Anaxis began, "and he was still breathing. There was an arrow in his chest." Benedict held up a bloody and broken wooden arrow. "I got it out and we found one of their archers in the tree, shooting from the treetop. He had gotten Henry as he walked by. We tried to find him but he had escaped."

Benedict threw the mangled arrow to the ground. He went up to join the rest of the men. "I think as soon as we got him on the horse and started heading back is when the breathing stopped. I know now, he is no longer with us. So we shall take this body back, and we shall honor it!" The men, beat down and tired, still suddenly burst out into a cheer, and the resilient spirit of knighthood was at its finest.

With that, the horses and men, in one synchronized movement, took off to return to their town and let everyone know that their fight was over. Jovan felt a pride in his heart. He knew he had done his best. He had put everything he had into what he had done.

Henry, he knew, had left behind a wife and their three children. Henry's sons would one day faced what their father had, and they would understand. They would see how he had fought for them, how he had bled for them, and how he had died protecting their town. It was always a somber moment for the knights to lose a brother in arms.

Jovan knew, that when he fought, other men had died that were not his colors.

The men that had died would always wane on his conscience. It would always be there in his mind that they had died at his own hand. It was the price he had to pay for honor and to uphold his name. To be a knight was to be a mythical legend for all the people to admire. It was to be strong and elegant, noble and kind. It meant doing anything for your people and for your men. Being a knight was being able to handle pressure and have the whole world watching you, the town depending on you. It was in Jovan's heart to fight and to feed the hunger that was his pride. If this was his duty, his purpose for this life, he would try to fulfill it in the best way that he could.

Jovan was once again in the back of his group as they headed for the town. They were way ahead of him. He rode solitary from the carnage as he tried to calm his mind, take all the air into his lungs, and thank God that he had survived.

In the blackness of the night, Jovan was suddenly shaken like never before-A large blow from behind, a force out of nowhere, he had been hit. All of his bones rattled, all of the sounds were a dull part of the background. The ringing in his ears were like cacophony of sirens, begging to him to stay with it, not let himself go, not give up the fight. Jovan could not help it as blackness filled his sight, and in one solid movement, he hit the ground.

He could lie here, maybe, and his blood would become part of the downtrodden earth. He could crawl back to town, his pride washed away with cowardice. But Jovan looked up into the face of a man high on a hazel stallion, and his blood ran cold.

"Get up!" Samuel yelled, violently, as he put the edge of his sword in Jovan's face. A beam of light glared off it from the moon above, a beam of light pointing right down to his chest. "Get up and face me," he demanded. Jovan's adrenaline flooded throughout him, a smothering warmth that caused him to shut out the shock and turn to fight mode.

He felt dehumanized while also feeling a surge go through him- it was an emotion that was hard to explain. He knew he would have to fight again, and he never wanted to fight. However, fighting was what he did best, and he began to prepare himself.

Here, in the dark forest, he would face his enemy, and maybe their fate would be settled here, he thought He knew it was bound to happen at some point- he would fight Samuel and hopefully this would all be settled and put behind them. Jovan was not scared to fight Samuel; but he feared losing his honor, as he would fight a man he had always defended and been on his side.

This was his brother in arms, the one he had always fought beside. But Jovan was not going to die at his hand, after surviving so many other things. Jovan never would have thought he would fight his own teammate. Jovan never thought he would be knocked off his horse. But he knew all battles stemmed from somewhere and just like any other, he could not back down.

Jovan forced himself back up. Samuel had gotten off his horse and approached Jovan. He began to swing his sword at him as Jovan, just in time, returned the motion.

Samuel had wild eyes. He was like a ravenous animal that had found his prey. He had such resentment in his motions. He fought Jovan with every fiber of his being. Jovan was worn down, his side was injured from being hit with the mace during the fight earlier that day. He felt an ache anytime he moved a muscle. But, just like before, there was no time to dwell on his injuries.

"Samuel," Jovan breathed. He backed away, and they now stood to face one another. "I will not fight another man who fights beside me." "Samuel paced around him, insanity still in his eyes, his presence was robust but certainly not dominant. Jovan would never let him win.

"This is our fight," Samuel replied. His voice was brute. "And we will settle it tonight." As he tried to take another swing at Jovan, Jovan backed away again. "I back away from you, Samuel, not because of fear, but because of honor. I will not fight a man with the same colors as I wear." Samuel stood for a second and stared into his rival. He had so obviously forgotten what it was like to be a human, and an archaic passion had overtaken him. "You have to understand, Jovan, that I will marry Gracie. And when I do, you will never see her again. She is betrothed to me. And I have every intention to go forward with the marriage. This is not over." Samuel went to get back on his horse, giving one more stoic look to Jovan. He then nudged his horse and galloped away, disappearing into the nightfall.

Chapter 3

Jovan now had nothing but time to think. He constantly thought about the beatings his body had endured; he thought about the emotional torture so many people had put him through. He knew that, tonight, he would face another sleepless night filled with blackness and thoughts of them all. Those people he had left behind had shaped his life in so many ways. Some had bent him, some had broken him, some had lifted him up. And in the hardest times, days like today, it seemed everyone was against him.

Some had loved him, some had destroyed him. Jovan had been shaken and broken and put back together into the iron prince everyone knew him as. Gracie had kind of done both. Jovan was not a stranger to love; in fact, he was just the opposite. But he knew the two of them would never know one another like they should. It was because of the man whose sword he had just faced, the man who saw him no differently and no more worthy than dust.

He rode home in silence. The night was completely quiet; the town was quiet as he returned. His beautiful horse carried him, just like always, to his humble house outside the city. If he had been born in a different time, in a different place, his life would not have taught him so much. He would not have been in such a tangle of emotion, he would not have known so much about himself. Jovan's love affair with knighthood had torn him to pieces. He wondered if the shallow things he fought for would make him whole again.

He knew, in the back of his mind, that he would keep fighting.

His journey was a story to tell; right now, it was an open book, but he kept adding pages, carefully, lovingly, piece by piece. It was time for a new chapter. It was time to move on. He knew he could end this. He could overcome the rivalry he had with Samuel, and he knew, that no matter what Samuel said, he would see her again.

Jovan was ok with his conscience as he knew that he had been the most honorable; he had backed down when he could have fought and ended it all tonight. Now, things were different. He had met his love and he had purpose. Though they may never end up together, he knew he would make it last as long as he could. He would fight for her, if nothing else, because he knew that she was worth it.

In that dark forest, no one would know what had really happened. No one would ever imagine that Samuel would turn against his brethren and fight. So many things that had been called noble had been tainted by the flaws of humanity. And there was nothing anyone else could do- these were the things knights worked out amongst themselves.

His bed below the window seemed to provide no comfort for him. His aching body and his racing mind had no mercy as he tried to find sleep, he did not know if he would ever find it.

Day break was upon him before he knew it. He had managed to sleep a little. He hoped nothing more would come of the incident with Samuel-could he still rely on Samuel to fight beside him? And it was also a dishonor to the king. Samuel had been like a son to the king, who had taken in he and his mother after Samuel's father had left them both. In order for a knight to turn on his fellow man, a vicious storm must have been brewing hard inside of him; the kind that makes one thoughtless, evil, and bitter- the kind that would drive any noble man to insanity.

But, Jovan hoped, this could maybe be fixed after all. The rivalry they had always had might have been what triggered it. Jovan just knew that when it came to Samuel, he would have to keep his guard up. It was not fear he had; it was not wanting to let Samuel get the upper hand. Jovan's power and resilience could outdo any enemy any day. But he did not want to have to use it.

Jovan had a sharp pain in his right side. An aching, dull, constant pain that was constantly reminding him of the carnage from yesterday. Upon lifting his shirt, a crimson pool had spread to cover almost the entire side of his body. The thin shirt that was covering it had been stained completely. It had all been a blur to him. His recent brush with brutality flashed before his eyes just then; a chaotic jumble of madness, shouting and bloodshed, arrows raining from the sky. Danger in every direction around him; and nowhere to run, but he would have never ran anyway. It was either conquer death or be conquered by it.

His armor, he knew, had been damaged from the blow he had received. The sterling metal he wore to protect himself had caved in and appeared so fragile now. Now, it seemed, this armor was just a false hope, like it was never protecting him in the first place.

Could his armor be stronger than he? Could the layer of metal he relied on and trusted with his life be enough to guard him, to defend him when he was inches away from an enemy wishing death upon him? He had seen the dents and the cracks, and he knew that this could have very well been his own flesh.

He knew he could not face another battle with his armor like this; and he would have to take it into town and have it repaired. He dreaded going into the town and facing all the people. He would have to face them and accept their congratulations on his victory. The girls would approach him, the people would greet him; they would cheer for him and expect to see a smile on his face. They would see him and think they were looking at a legend, and he would have to uphold that image they all had of him- when on the inside, he did not feel like any of those things. He did not feel like he could face them all right now-because all he felt was pathetic.

Jovan pulled himself up off the bed and took off his ruined shirt. He threw it to the floor and went to his wardrobe to search for another. He was sort of a lucky man. He had plenty of clothes. He had a decent house, not a big house, but decent, and he always had food when he needed it. In this world of adversity he was certainly blessed. He was a prosperous man- he never went without food or shelter. He was either looking up, thanking God for all his blessings and bounty, or down on his knees, begging him for just one more day.

As Jovan stumbled toward the door of his house he had to stop to clutch his aching side. This was a brand new day, a brand new beginning, and brand new problems to be faced with. Injury was not something he needed right now.

Jovan did not have to worry though; he could count on his horse to carry him wherever he needed to go. He clumsily, while still holding to his side, climbed up on the animal's back and headed in the direction of his renaissance town.

This morning, the sun sat high above the trees and crowned the earth's edges. Jovial, peaceful rays of light stretched through the sky. Brightness flashed through the morning to make the world seem lighter. The calm light reflected down on the once dreadful earth. Dew danced on the grass. Though early, the air was already on his shoulders like a thick blanket. It was the kind of heat that made it hard to breathe. He was sweating immensely in his saddle and it covered his entire body. He needed to get his armor fixed, go back to his house, and try to find some relaxation. Or should he? Thoughts raced through his mind. Jovan felt desperate to find an answer. He wanted to be the one who not only saved everyone else, but also himself. He knew he could never do that alone.

It was just all so exhausting. To ride high, and be struck low, and to lay and bleed on the earth, to be looked in the face by menacing men, to have a fight rage on within you forever. These were the things he struggled with the most. When it came to the world, Jovan stood tall upon it, and all who saw him looked up to see his glory. But Jovan knew that they were all just looking for an answer. He knew the answer was not within him, within any man for that matter; it was a far deeper truth, a truth that must be found as you make your journey in life. The sad part was, they would all continue to search in the wrong places; in places where war was the worst tyrant and they were all his subjects.

Today, as he slumped over on horseback as he held to his aching side, Jovan knew that he had been weakened. It was a startling blow to his golden reputation. Jovan could see the first few buildings as he entered town. There was a church, a few houses, and lots of booths and tables for the merchants in the marketplace for selling goods and services. If he continued through the town, he would pass the main farms, and the street leading straight through the main square lead straight to the majestic castle, the landmark of the town, the most breathtaking structure Jovan's eyes had ever met. Lights and music, royalty, people from towns and worlds away-there was nothing else like it. He knew he had been a part of it all. He knew he had been masked by the vanity and the ways of their world. The world belonging to the castle and the world belonging to the town were completely separate from one another.

Yet, he was part of them both.

Jovan's ashen horse carried him into the town. The blacksmith was at the outskirts of town. He steered the horse in that direction. The horse walked lazily into the crowd. People were all around, though it was early. The townspeople saw as Jovan passed, some would stop and wave to him, some would smile at him and politely move out of his way. Some would stop to talk to him, they would all tell him how great he was. The only words Jovan could find were 'thank you,' weak words that held no weight compared to what their words meant to him.

"Sire Jovan!" The blacksmith greeted Jovan as he approached the booth. The blacksmith, an old man that had done nothing but metal work his entire life, stood aging behind his booth. His gray beard and tortured hands reflected his lifetime of work. He had always made Jovan's armor. He had crafted the art that protected his precious body, he knew every muscle, every curve of his sturdy frame. He knew the way to make the metal strong, but make it light.

"My good sir," Jovan replied. He handed in the broken piece, dented in and crushed like a broken dream. "I got a bad blow in battle. I was hoping you could fix it." Jovan got a genuine smile in return. "One of the best soldiers around will certainly need his armor fixed the best way possible. I'll do it for you. No charge!" "Thank you my good man, I could never ask for a better service."

"When you were fighting last night, is that when this happened?" Jovan nodded, a somber look on his face. He did not want to revisit his thoughts on the battle from yesterday. "it was a brutal fight. But just like every fight, we got through it, and I know we will do it over again." Jovan would like to say his yesterdays did not define him, but he would be wrong. The burden he carried on his shoulders was all from the past. He knew he was slowly starting to become it.

The man held up the damaged piece of armor, and inspected it. "Looks like a nasty fight," he stated, "I'll need to spend some extra time on this." The man scratched his head, thinking. "Give me an hour. I'll need my best tools and my best skills." He gave Jovan a wink. Jovan let out a smile. This man, despite his age, despite his adversity, despite the job he had helping nobles live the lives they had, was always in a happy place and never was he angered by his job. He was consumed in his work and had made it his life. "Sire Jovan, you will be wearing this again in no time. And I'll put in some extra reinforcement to make it extra strong."

In the distance, across the town square, Jovan could feel a set of eyes on him. The eyes were alluring, and he could feel their energy from where he stood. They followed him with every move he made.

He was immediately drawn to where the stare was coming from and immediately found himself gazing into a suntanned face framed with crimson hair. He was staring right at River. A smile began to overtake her face as she realized she had been discovered. Her smile brightened as a flower would bloom, her eyes lit up as an ember would turn to flame.

Jovan turned back to face his blacksmith. "Thank you my good man," he stated, "I'll be back later to pick it up."

Jovan headed over to her. It was almost like a trance, like he was being drawn over. As he approached, the air seemed to become hotter and hotter, heating up to a thousand degrees. An inferno was brewing inside her, he could tell, burning her from the inside to be let out. And when she spoke, words scattered from her mouth like sparks from a lighter.

"Jovan," she breathed, "it is so nice to run into you." Jovan never knew what to say to River-it was hard to say anything that did not give her the wrong idea. "Yes, I had to come and have my armor fixed," he replied. This seemed to fuel her even more; her smile was feverish. "I was hoping to find you here. I wasn't looking for you or anything, I just thought you might be in town today. And as it turns out, I was right!" Jovan let out a nervous laugh. The desire River had burned into him, he knew what she was longing for. She reached out to grab his hand. "I wish we could have another night like the one we shared at the dance."

Jovan feared that he may have given River the wrong idea- letting her get close was falling into her trap; it was a black widow's web of mesmerizing lust and an entanglement of hypnotic passion.

It took him a second to find the right words for her- but he knew that was not possible.

"River, dancing with you was nice. I can't see you today, though. I have to get back home after my armor is fixed. The fight has taken a toll on me. My side got hurt and I have to get some rest."

River let go of Jovan's hand and began to focus on the slight bloody tinge that was beginning to spread across his shirt. She gently put her hand upon it. "Jovan, only the best would do this for his town. The strongest and most noble. I'm so glad to know you, Sire Jovan. Come and let me cheer you up." Jovan pulled away from her. He was a noble man, but River's advances had been really getting to him. "River, you are such a nice girl. But today, I can't go with you."

As soon as Jovan got his words out, he caught a glimpse of something up ahead of him. A glimpse of white, a quick blur through his line of vision. He altered his gaze to look past River and that was when he saw her-she was cutting through a crowd of people, clad in flowing white, a mystical entity that stood out from the otherwise dull crowd. Jovan knew immediately that it was Gracie.

"I have to go, River, I'll see you later," He hastily blurted out, and he rapidly started working his way toward her, his gigantic horse being led behind him. As he approached her he could see that she was alone. She had a basket that she was putting fruit in, fruit that she was buying from a merchant as she stood and conversed with the seller. Jovan was watching her from afar, he felt foolish for this-he had never had to chase a lady like this, they had always been drawn to him, and he would then choose whether or not he wanted to liaison with them.

But Gracie was different. Her presence was gentle and powerful, lingering and sweet. Just to be around her made Jovan feel brighter-it made him feel renewed, like a whole new world had opened up for him, like the person he had been before never mattered-because she offered him a new sense of meaning. He thought twice before approaching her-not only was she a bit intimidating, he did not want the townspeople to see them together, to get the wrong idea and cause suspicion. But Jovan knew that if he did not talk to her today it would bother him in his sleep, it would forever stay in the back of his mind. He could never forgive himself for not giving an effort.

In one smooth motion, Jovan found himself walking over to her. As she was turning from the fruit stand, she spotted him there as he approached. "Jovan!" She exclaimed, her face and tone full of pure joy. He was slightly relieved at her reaction. "Hello again, Gracie," he greeted, trying to hide his smile. His heart had faded into his being, his whole body a pulsing vessel. The white dress she wore gave off an elegant and angelic feel, her alabaster skin was glowing and her periwinkle eyes sparked as she smiled. She spotted Jovan's horse, still being led behind him, and ran to start petting it between the ears. She grabbed an apple from her basket and began to feed the animal. "Your horse is so beautiful," she stated, laughing as the horse stuck his nose in her basket, searching for more. Jovan felt speechless. He did not know what he was doing, he did not know why he was trying like he was. He would never have Gracie as his own, he would never share with her the things he so longed for, he would never get to show her the truly beautiful person that he was.

He was saddened at these things; he knew it was truly a shame. He knew she would never be loved the way she deserved. And now, standing here in the town square with her, he felt all these things at once, and an overwhelming feeling of sadness seemed to overtake him.

But as she spoke, he found happiness again and soon got lost in the velvet words. "I can take you for a ride if you want." Jovan's words spilled out before he could even process them. "Leave your basket here. You can pick it up when I get my armor." Gracie was speechless for a minute. She looked down at the fruit, back at the horse, and back to Jovan again. She turned to the merchant running the booth she was at. "May I ask you to hold this fruit for me?" she began, "I have to come pick it up later." And before even getting a response, she turned back to Jovan with a smile. "Ok let's go!" She stated.

Jovan, in a trance of a thousand emotions, got up on the majestic animal's back, and offered his large hand down to help her up. She swung up on the saddle behind him, and held tight to his sides. He was trembling from disbelief, from knowing that she was indeed here with him, but he did not see how this could be true. Any girl he had ever wanted had been so easy to reach, and though she was here, she still seemed too far away for him. She was not here on this horse for him. She was here for herself, because she loved these things, she loved the small things in life in general. This is one of the most beautiful things Jovan had ever experienced.

Gracie laughed as Jovan nudged the horse forward, and set into a full canter. She was like a dream, her hair occasionally brushing up on his shoulder as they ran far away from all the people. No one else in the world would matter right now anyway. He did not know where they were going, he did not know what would happen once they got there. But Jovan did not care. Any second like this was enough for him.

Jovan found himself going back toward the forest. He knew the area would be torn apart, shredded to pieces from the battle that had taken place. He knew that dead men probably still occupied the now peaceful woods, as they lay resting quietly in a solace that only they belonged to. Knowing this, he turned to take a different path-the one that led to the ocean.

Their town, though also blooming with forest and farmland, was about an hour from the coast on horseback. Most of the town's business took place here. There were merchants and traders that spent their entire lives on the sea. It was a beautiful place, Jovan loved to come here. At the right place, away from the business and chaos, there was a private beach, secluded from most of the world. The white capped waves would beat relentlessly against the brown cliffs, restless and angry. The calming whisper of the wind kept him from escaping reality as it was sometimes chilling, but usually relaxing and quiet. Just like the courtyard at the castle, he knew this was perfect-it was just the two of them and they could escape together for awhile.

"I know a perfect place," Jovan shouted behind his shoulder, as they continued on horseback. Gracie was still back there and holding to him. She had been clinging tightly to his muscled frame and laughing from behind him as they would speed up at times. "Take me where you want to go," she said. And so they headed to the beach.

When they got to the beach, it was just as Jovan had remembered it in his mind. He had never taken another girl here. The girls in his past had all been the same, swooning over him, begging for him, and yet he had no desire to do these things with them. But Gracie made him feel like he should always improve his next move, like he had to be good enough for her. But when they were together, things were easy.

They sat by a cluster of boulders near the shore. Jovan's horse wondered off to get some grass as they sat to talk.

"Next week is when the wedding will be," she started. "I am not prepared-our lives will be so different, and I have hardly any time to get ready for it." Jovan was silent. This was the one thing he had forgotten-he had let Samuel escape his mind, but as soon as he realized it again, everything seemed tainted. This was not real, this was not ever going to matter-because in one week, She would be wed to him, and she would be for the rest of her life.

"I don't understand how you can learn to love someone you are arranged to be with," Jovan started, "I don't think Samuel cares. Having a beautiful girl is all that matters to him anyway." Gracie did not respond. Jovan sighed and looked to the sand.

"Samuel is a good man. He gets carried away with himself sometimes," She finally said. "I know I am lucky to be with him.

Knights are some of the most noble and beautiful people around. And I think my father wanted to give me to a knight of Hawthorne just to make amends. But war is still going on. And now my betrothed is fighting against the men of the town I came from. I will have to learn to accept these things." Jovan had never seen her in this way, he had never thought about the things which she faced each day. It was more of a struggle than anyone realized. "There are good men in this town, too," he began, "but to go against your town is never easy. I could never do it. After fighting for this place and nearly dying for it, I know that this town is the one I will always be a part of." Jovan always knew that the town had molded him more than it should have. It had taken more of him than he would have liked to give away. But his loyal blood kept him fighting and kept him pushing through to protect this place.

"The knights in this town are so noble. They are so loyal to their town and they fight with their best. I admire that about this place." She smiled as she said this. Jovan smiled too. "Gracie, you are the most noble I have met. And no matter what happens, I am so glad to have met you."

Jovan knew that even if he lost her forever, even if he was condemned for seeing another man's woman, he would never regret it. Suddenly, a feeling of want came over him-he had in his mind he could never let her go. He had in his mind he wanted to experience the most intimate and darkest parts of her, and share forbidden emotion.

Their conversation lasted until the stars began to show themselves, until the ocean birds had long flown back to their crude nests. The talk waned into the night, with desire burning more and more into him, searing him from the inside out. And suddenly, as he found himself drawing closer, he kissed her.

The kiss was hypnotic; it was like Jovan had found his kryptonite. He could have gone on forever. But before he knew it, they lay on the beach together. The moon casted a lunar glow on the both of them, and their clothes were the only thing separating them from their darkest desires. Coming up for air, Gracie breathed out a brief statement, "Don't be afraid to make me yours." And Jovan did just that.

Sin was so delightful at night. It seemed that night blanketed it all from the rest of the world, the night would swallow it up and it would not matter anymore. The lonely feeling of night made his longing a little bit stronger.

Sweet was her tongue and her lips. Her skin was alabaster that was warm with every touch. He ran his large callused hand down her waist, down her leg, and he swam in the azure pools that were her eyes. He could forget to come up for air, he thought; and he might drown.

He was now the purest he had ever been. Naked and vulnerable his two worlds met-his strength and resilience and such a beautiful part of him that was made with desire and ecstasy. There was never enough, never enough closeness, never enough time between the two of them. No matter how much time there was the want never went away.

And now, it seemed, time was their enemy. They had one week until the wedding. Jovan knew they had loved one another since the start. But Gracie and Samuel had no love. He never saw how incredible everything was about her. He was afraid she would get lost one day in the monotony that her life would surely be, as a house wife with a Husband that needed to uphold his status in society. He would wear his wedding band in vain as it would just be a status symbol and the marriage would be fruitless. Jovan would not be allowed to love her. But he knew he could not turn away that easy.

Jovan's bliss was a time warp of fantasy and being higher than he had ever been. It was better than any drunken feeling he had had, better than any adrenaline rush that had ever pulsed through him. It was like a beautiful mistake, he knew. It was the most fulfilled he had ever been, yet he knew that what he had done had been unspeakable for someone like him. He would have never touched another man's woman, especially a man he fought beside. But he knew, down in his heart, that she was the only thing that could fix the broken pieces and make him whole again.

"Gracie," he breathed as they lay shrouded in darkness, "I wish I could marry you." Gracie lay in silence. Jovan swore he would never say anything like that to a woman. That was before he knew love like this existed. Their sexy liaison had led them to an eternal bond and he knew he would never forget. He wished they could run away together. If times had been different, if he was not a loyal soldier, if he was not with another man's woman, maybe they could have. But like Jovan had known from before-time was not on their side.

The lull of crashing waves was constant. He was so close to the ocean. And, just at that moment, he began to also hear familiar rain as it collided on to their flesh. Silence was their bliss as the rain came mercilessly down upon them. It hit them as it hit the earth, for they were not superior. Just like the earth, they one day would waste away and life around them would go on. Jovan felt like he was the same as the dirt. He felt worthless and sorry and sinful. He felt that he deserved to be out in the rain. But the girl of his dreams was in his arms.

"Jovan," she finally replied, "this is a sad thing for the both of us. Our love will go wasted. But don't worry. The sea is jealous and the sky weeps for us."

Chapter 4

Jovan's soul had never endeavored such love. He had loved with a love that was more than he could have ever imagined- it was a white-knuckled holding on kind of feeling; It was loving another person more than he loved himself, it was a menagerie of wild thoughts in his mind. His muscles were numb to feeling, his aura floated high above the clouds. He hoped that maybe he would fall and land hard and be shaken back to earth.

Jovan was not meant to fall this hard or love this freely. If he was anything like he was supposed to be, he would never let a person get to him this way. He would have a hard exterior, he would fight for his people and he would keep up appearances, and he would continue to be longed for but he would never give in.

But Jovan often found himself down paths he should not be on, he often found himself wanting more from the shallow life he led. Jovan was full of passion and full of hope for a lifetime companion. He had so much more living to do, he had so much to share with another person. He was bred to be a knight but he was led to be a lover. All of the things that Jovan was made up of were beautiful.

And he knew, you can't hide from the beautiful things that you are.

Jovan had given a big part of himself to her. It was not like the other girls- for her, he had really opened up. He had let his guard down and gave in and romanced her with all the love he had. He had never given so much love to another person, but he felt that everything was so right about it.

Jovan had done it-he had romanced an angel. She was so much higher than him. She flew high above the clouds, she shone with the sun rays as they beat down upon him during all his days. She was a priceless piece of artwork he would have otherwise never touched. His lips, his skin, his hands, and his heart had all touched her tonight.

Jovan breathed out loud. "My armor," he said, suddenly. "I forgot about my armor back in town. I never picked it up. And you left your fruit." Gracie laughed. "Well looks like we will be running into one another in town again," she replied. Jovan knew they would have to leave from here soon because if they waited much longer, daylight would be upon them.

By now the rain had stopped. The earth and sand was wet, however, and the summer air became sticky on his skin.

As Gracie lay with her head on Jovan's chest, she began to touch the tender broken skin that had come from his injury. He let out a slight groan as she touched it. His large callused hands grabbed hers and held it there, as he did not want her to pay attention to his battle wound.

"What happened to you," she asked nonchalantly. "It was the fight," he replied, "I got hit. I almost got knocked to the ground. It was what had messed up my armor, and what had led me to come to town and run into you." Gracie slid down and gave the area a kiss. "Brave soldier," she said, "don't be too brave for your own good."

Jovan held back a laugh at that. Plenty of times, he had done just that. Jovan's mind was not wired to process death as being a possibility. For him, death was winning and losing, it was strong and weak. He was way past being brave. Jovan was fearless.

But there was no way he would tell her what Samuel had done. He never wanted her to know Samuel's flaws, that he was more of a fighter than a lover; because, he figured, he had already done so much to hurt Samuel already. Though Samuel had threatened to fight him, Jovan saw no bounds for what it would take to get to her- he would do whatever it would take.

They were huddled together- every part of them touching. Jovan could feel her breath on his skin, he could feel her heart beat, a metronome to the epitome of his very existence.

"Come on Gracie, We have to get back to town. I know it is late, but we should get back before anyone sees us." She lay there a second more, then finally set up and began to stand. "yes, the night is already gone, and we have been out here for hours," she said. Jovan had to walk a few feet in the dark to spot his horse. The animal was well trained, it had not gone anywhere without its master. Jovan grabbed him and got back on, offering an arm down to her, who then joined him.

They galloped under a million glistening stars. The sky shone like malachite. The sky was always changing around him, yet the earth seemed to stand still. Time seemed to stand still. Though it seemed to be about an hour, they had been gone for half the night.

Jovan's thoughts revolved around being spotted. If anyone should see the two of them riding together at this time of night, now early morning, word would quickly get around town. Jovan knew he had sinned. He knew she was Samuel's bride but he could never see her that way. She seemed so free, like never belonging to anyone.

If Samuel knew that Jovan had slept with Gracie there would be blood. Royal, noble, rich, red blood of two different breeds would be spilled throughout their kingdom. The court would probably have something to do with it, as they would not want a knight that could not uphold his nobility. The two men would certainly face one another and the outcome of that would be uncertain. And though Jovan was not afraid, he never wanted to cause any problems or ruin his spotless reputation, let alone Gracie's reputation.

Jovan had a vision of the river running red, in a still and silent forest where the song birds ceased to sing. It was a war-torn land where prosperity used to reign. And the war was because of him and his foolish heart.

He knew he would have to get these thoughts out of his mind. He had done something so beautiful and so tempting. He could never find joy in the two of them if he continued to guilt himself.

"Thank you for this evening," Jovan suddenly said back to Gracie after a few solid minutes of silent galloping. "It was everything I dreamed of." Gracie held to Jovan tighter. He knew that she now had a part of him that he hoped she would put far away in her heart and keep it sacred forever.

Jovan and Gracie together were taboo but they were so right in every other way. As they neared the town, sunset slowly started to break through. This would be perfect because it would seem that they had just each gotten to town early rather than had stayed out all night. Upon reaching the outskirts, Jovan stopped his horse. "We have to get off here," he started, "so no one will see us together and suspect anything." Gracie jumped off the horse and looked up at Jovan.

"I know we have just met one another, but I feel like you are like no one else I have ever known," Jovan added. Gracie gave him a deep look, one that went deeper than just his exterior. "I feel like that too, Jovan. And I loved every minute of it. I hope I will see you again." Gracie took Jovan's hand once more and gave it a kiss, then began walking toward the town. Jovan decided to wait a minute before going right behind her. Jovan turned toward the forest again, because right before entering the forest was the river from his vision earlier. He decided to let his horse drink.

He knew town would not be open for about another hour. But Jovan also knew that if he went home he would be alone with his thoughts. Jovan had guilt for the night's events. But he also had very much fulfillment. The thought of what he had done gave him so much power. He felt he could fight a dozen wars on his own right at this moment, and he did not care what happened. He knew that if he died tomorrow he had touched the face of Heaven and he had found the feeling he had always searched for.

As the sun found its way over the horizon and the forest came alive, Jovan picked himself up from the tree he had propped up on. He grabbed his horse and went ahead into town. Today, he would accept their stares and their handshakes. This time, he would not hesitate to smile.

The old blacksmith was at work today as always, working hard just like any other day. His face lit up when he saw Jovan. "Sire Jovan! I was wondering if you would make it today. I finished your armor yesterday." The man turned and grabbed a masterpiece, it looked unlike any of Jovan's old armor. But it was, it was his entire bodice that had been reconstructed. The metal was polished and shined. There was a beautiful and elegant design that had been engraved on the piece. It was a design with sparrows, etched in gold- one on each side of his broad chest piece.

"Thank you, very much, this is so much more than I expected," he gasped. "Please let me pay you something." The man shook his head. "No sire, what you do for this town is more than enough. You like it?" Jovan shook his head. "It looks amazing," he answered.

He looked at the sparrows with a hopeful glance, these birds would someday uphold his honor. At this thought, he blushed. His honor, he now knew, was somewhat tainted; but he somehow felt like more of a man now and he accepted the armor.

"Are you alright, Sire?" The blacksmith peered at Jovan, the blushing was obvious. He nodded to his friend. "doing well, just tired," Jovan stated. He wanted nothing more suddenly than to get out of here and escape the now accumulating crowd around him in the town.

"Thank you again for your fine work," he stated, and at that, he strapped the new armor on his horse and began to finally head home.

Just as Jovan turned to leave, he felt a firm tap on the shoulder. When he felt the warmth radiating throughout his body, he knew exactly who could be behind him.

"River," he stated, shocked. The look on her face was stoic and her arms akimbo. The balmy summer heat was cornering them in a tight and huddled crowded street. River's scorching eyes permeated him, a thousand unforgiving needles. Her look was unsettling. A blistering presence, she was dressed in scarlet red and the auburn hair tumbled down her shoulders. She appeared so reckless, so demanding, so fierce.

"Jovan, I need to talk with you," she started again. Jovan began to turn away again. He would try to blow her off, he thought. "Jovan, you need to hear this. You want to hear this. Trust me." Jovan's heart began to skip every other beat. Maybe she somehow knew about what he and Gracie had done. Maybe, he feared, others knew it too.

Maybe their liaison had not gone unnoticed. Jovan feared River had witnessed his late- night rendezvous.

"Ok River, I can take the time to talk to you. But I must get home soon. We need to go somewhere no one else can hear us." Jovan feared his business being victim to prying ears.

River gave him a slight smile. It was not like the smiles she usually gave him. There was something behind this. There was such ruthless emotion behind the look she gave. He was a bullet and her hot-headed disposition was the loaded gun.

They walked back to where Jovan was before, at the quiet brook in the opening of the forest. Jovan felt as if he was not actually walking the whole way here. He felt he had picked himself up and carried himself here. He did not know if she knew what he thought she knew. But if she did, she had information that could detriment him greatly.

River was the kind of girl that would give you a good time and move on from. But, she would always be in the back of your mind, and she would always be there on lonely nights. A good time from her would always turn into pleasurable sin. It was the kind of sin you could forgive yourself for, the kind that might make you smile years down the road. It was nothing serious, she would never break your heart- but you would treasure your time with her and she would teach you so much about yourself. You could nod and smile at her in public but always remember the way you had held one another and wanted one another. The want was the worst part. Wanting was the predecessor to sin. It was the act that led to it all. To want was to have, and to have was to only want more.

Jovan tried to prop himself up by another tree. But River got right in front of him, and led him to the tree instead, and pinned him against it. He was trapped in a blazing fire now.

"Jovan, I noticed you came back to town the same time as Gracie today. And I know you left with her yesterday. You left from me to talk to her." Jovan felt River was attacking him. He did not owe her an explanation. He did not have to tell her anything. And suddenly, he was angry and frustrated. He was tired of her getting to him. He was tired of her manipulating him.

"River, don't get involved in my personal business." Jovan had immediately shut down. He wanted her to know as little as possible, because he knew she could not be trusted. River's face fell from menacing to desperate.

"Jovan," She grabbed his shirt. She was holding tight to it. "Please, actually talk to me. Tell me something. What do you like so much about her?"

She clung to him with all her strength. He saw how her desire still burned for him. She was a torch and wanted him to be the everlasting flame. Jovan knew he could never give her that.

"River, we get along so well. She understands me. She understands the..." he trailed off, "the way I have to be." The way he had to be was tough but also a lover. He would never show that side of himself to anyone else. River would never be able to get that.

Her eyes pleaded to his words. The reality was, she could never have him like Gracie had had him. And though she hated it, she had to accept it. She had to accept the truth.

"River you are an amazing friend. I am so glad to know you. You are a beautiful person. And I don't want you to think less of me because I violated Gracie's engagement."

"Samuel is not like you." She finally said after what seemed like an eternity of silence. "Samuel would never be able to love and fight with an equal amount of passion. I know you are much more of a man than he is."

Had he always been a man? Or had Gracie made him a man? Or had it been knighthood? Maybe he was never a man in the first place- maybe he liked to think he had been to build up the ego his mind.

"Samuel is a great fighter but he is not a person that is so easy to love. Gracie likes you because you are so real."

Jovan shrugged. He never saw himself this way. He wondered if this was how everyone else saw him too. "River, I'm sorry. I guess you wanted to be with me. But I can't lie to you. I can't lie to myself like that. I know it is not what you wanted but there is someone out there that can give you what I can't."

At this point, River's eyes were flooding with glassy tears. Maybe he should have watched his words a little more carefully.

"Yes, I wanted to be with you, I want you to see me like you see Gracie. And when I saw the two of you come back together, I didn't know what to think. I thought maybe we would have a chance together, because you know, the dance-"

"River, I have messed up. What I did can never be known. Gracie and I will be over soon. After she is married, none of what we did will have any weight on this world. And I have to rely on you to keep it all a secret." Jovan interrupted, not willing to hear anything more about the dance that had started this whole thing.

River, still crying, nodded without saying a word. "Jovan," she breathed, "we will find a way to make this right." Jovan felt so desperate. He wanted so badly for River to forgive him. But he also wanted her to accept the truth. He knew he had created a mess and he knew he was now responsible for cleaning it all up.

"You can go now," she said angrily, "I don't need to say anything else to you."

River disappeared into the feverish heat of summer. He prayed for summer wind to give him the ability to breathe again. She walked until he could no longer see her. He did not move a muscle. Why was it so hard for him to love? Why was it so hard for people to accept his love?

Strangely, it was not hard for him to accept it. Though he knew it was forbidden, it was still everything he had ever wanted and though he would only get a brief taste of their sweet affair it would be the pinnacle of all the things he had ever done in his life.

River had passed through his life at different points. He knew that Gracie would be there for him always. When he would see her in town or at the royal gatherings, he knew that no matter what She would look over and smile at him and they would always remember the time that they had had. It would be something only they would share, because no one else would ever know and no one would ever find out.

Jovan finally made it home that day. He was exhausted. He tried his armor on but the heavy metal put such pressure on his injured side. Jovan wondered if he would ever be the same again. He wondered if he would be able to be strong like he used to be. What if this situation took the last ounce of strength that he had? He might begin to waste away, he thought, he might finally go away to nothing. He could not fathom the fact that River knew his darkest and most precious secret. He would never be able to forgive himself for letting her find out.

Jovan had been living his life mostly under the night sky and sleeping whenever he had the chance. He took off the clothes he had worn for the day and found his bed under the window. And though the sun shone bright and the world outside of here was very much alive, Jovan quickly went into a deep sleep.

When Jovan awakened, it was dusk in the town. He felt energized and back to his normal self. Jovan knew that he was strong, and his strength would be everlasting. It was all he had. The ability to fight, the ability to uphold such tremendous valor, the ability to never stop looking toward the sky in the hopes that someday what he was doing would be good for something. Jovan's hope had gotten him through many things.

His mistake had been the other part of him-the amorous, passionate, curious part. How flawed was his being? How could a warrior of his caliber be so human?

Chaos seemed to take place in the town in the few days after that. The people seemed to be on edge. The air around them had changed. There was now an unsettling vibe around them, they had all been fearing the worst. There was word that there may be another attack on the town, that Januvia had still not given up.

One day, a falcon had flown into town to deliver a note. The gigantic, gallant bird had soared as a black shadow through Hawthorne's skies, and landed wings- folded on the top of their king's castle. This bird was from Januvia and a note had been tied to one leg.

Upon receiving the note, word got around that an attack may be soon taking place. The king had issued a warning for the knights to be ready in the case of anything happening. Jovan felt no emotion upon hearing this. Fighting was nothing new to him now. It was a part of his life. He felt he would face all his days like they were a dream, foggy and nonexistent, yet still fighting to get through.

His pure ecstasy had been blocked out due to the realization that time was not on his side. He was now facing nothing but time, as the wedding was only days away. Time would only close doors for him now, making him nothing but a memory to vanished eras that were so far gone. He knew that a wedding should be the furthest thing from his mind right now with talk of war. But the matters of his heart would always stay in the forefront of his mind.

Wartime would soon sweep over his now peaceful town. There would be invasions, men that were afraid and men that were not. For days they would fight until they could fight no longer. For that time, nothing but war would reign. The most human thing about them would be the possibility of death.

He used to be so eager for life and so eager to become the legend that he was now. But it was nothing like he ever thought it would be. He was a fighter and he was good at what he did. He was loved by all the people in his town. But he had never been so alone, after having the most amorous desire for the most captivating angel he had ever known, she could now never be his again.

It was then that he knew-he had to see her again.

Jovan had finally found rest over the past few days. He had been alone in his house in the woods. His thoughts, however, had kept him company. He was never one for being around people much. Jovan considered himself a loner, in a way- a man that was very private, a man that did not want to face everyone as they all had a need to interact with him, to fill him full of their petty words and put him high on a pedestal, because he never felt like he had been worth celebrating.

The falcon had flown in here across enemy lines. It had been a huge black shadow against the velvet sky, soaring in quietly as it had a job to do, to be loyal to the town it had came from. That Falcon could have encountered anything, arrows, other vicious animals, or even lightening shooting him down from the sky. But he had flown fearlessly into his enemy's town and done his job. He had been sent back with another note, a note the king and the court had spent hours on writing.

The note, though well-thought out, had only been a few sentences:

We will stand and face you, we will never lose our honor. We will fight until we can fight no more.

It had been scrawled neatly on the richest parchment paper, with a stamp from the Januvia king.

Hawthorne was such a prideful place. They would always stand up for their honor, they would never let anyone take that from them. Even if there was a fight they should not fight, they would still be there ready to face anything the war threw at them. This is why Jovan was the way that he was, this is why he was constantly putting himself through hell when he fought. He would rather die than lose his honor.

Jovan felt, because of his long hours of rest, that he had been nonexistent to the world for what only seemed to him a large amount of time. He woke up with completely different emotion than he had gone to sleep with. So much had happened to him since he had last found his bed. He had fought in a battle, he had slept with an untouchable maiden, and he had felt a thousand pounds of pressure hit him all at once when River admitted that she knew the truth.

Though he had escaped it for the time being, he would have to face it all eventually.

His side had now begun to heal. He was still sore upon moving, and stiff if he lay still long enough. But he could feel himself healing and once healed, his once injured side would be stronger than It ever was.

Jovan had thoughts about venturing out and trying to see her again. He hoped and prayed that he would run into her again, see her at the palace again, and, best of all- see her on the beach again, laying naked with him as she smiled, and they wasted away the entire night under one translucent moon.

He knew if he did see her again he would wish that he could have her and it would be hard to keep himself away. He knew that, now, he would have to tell himself no-and this would be the hardest part about seeing someone he had so much love for. He wanted to at least tell her goodbye and that he treasured the time they had had together. He wanted her to know the few times he had spent with her had been ingrained in his memory and he would never let it go.

If they could have been together, their days would all blend together into one single blissful lifetime, their hearts strong and their knees weak for one another always.

If his heart was solid and true, it would beat for her forever.

Jovan thought it was so beautiful that through everything, he was able to find love. In this town with adversity and sickness and brutal war, Jovan had still found something so beautiful. He knew that the love he had felt would never leave him. He felt if he had lost it, he would be nothing.

Jovan had never been a stupid creature. He was never weak. Jovan was complicated. No matter how strong he was, no matter how many times he would try and tell himself otherwise, that would never change.

Jovan had all he needed right now. He was a powerhouse. Why would he be any other way? God had crafted him with divine muscle, the epitome of beauty, and a rare breed of strength. God gave him a conscience and a brilliant mind, and everything he needed to live in this medieval world.

The fairytale that everyone knew had had his rest. Now he was ready to see what would come of his life-what would come of his fights, what would ever come of his solitary existence? He was ready to face the fight. He was ready to go into it with no second thoughts and live with the consequences.

A storm ravaged through the town later that day. The thunder growling menacingly through the blackened clouds, the lightening striking down upon them all- it was as if everything terrible had tried to hit earth all at once, and taunt its normality-it's peace, it's orbit. Thunder came down upon them like God had rolled a set of gargantuan dice, gambling on their well being.

The storm caused Jovan to feel awakened. The chaos going on outside so perfectly mirrored the chaos going on in his mind. He suddenly felt the storm beckon to him, he felt it awaken a longing inside of him. He was going to go find her.

If war broke out tomorrow, if he were to die, he would never get to tell her how he felt. So today, because he could not see into the future, he would go. Thunder, lightning, fire, and rain could never keep him away.

In Jovan's disillusioned mind, he could just walk out and she would be there waiting for him and they could just walk away from everything together. So that was what he did, he stumbled out of his house and faced the rain. He saw the blurry rain-soaked blackness ahead of him- one single sheet of black night, mysterious and hard as rock to break, because everything that tried to block it got swallowed up in it. Jovan was drenched with gallons of European rain, he could feel his senses magnify greatly. Jovan started to walk right into it. Large, pendulous drops of rain hit him all at once from all directions.

Suddenly, through the brutal wind and furious rain, Jovan could see faint shadows in the distance. As the shadows approached, he could see that there were men and horses- hundreds of them, and they were all headed his way. Just then, Jovan knew that it was a group, and they were angry, and they had malicious intent. Jovan knew that they were here to fight.

Jovan had seen the troops coming over. They had planned to attack and he had been the first ones to see them coming. Jovan turned to go back to his house, quietly escaping so as though not to draw attention to himself.

Would Jovan have to face them all on his own? Would he be killed and left to die alone, and no one would ever know? There was no time to get his horse-he knew he would need the animal, and he had never fought without it. But there was no time. Now, there was an army headed toward the town prepared to destroy everything in their path. And if they made it to the castle, they would destroy it too. Jovan knew he had to take it into his own hands. And somehow, he would have to let everyone else know so he would have backup.

Jovan ran into the trees. When he was in hiding, it was hard for him to run as fast and as stealthily as he needed. He could hear chaos, he could feel them all as they got closer with their weapons and their horses, and all he had with him was a bow and arrow, and once he ran out of arrows he would be unarmed.

Jovan was a mess- a physical and a mental mess. He knew that he could not fight at his best like this. But he also knew that he had to fight somehow. This is what it had come to.

Jovan ran, concealing himself behind the trees, blindly dodging what was in his way, the rain and wind torturing him the whole way. Jovan's sparrows guarded him, God guarded him. He had ran into battle before. He had faced it like he had faced all his yesterdays and all his tomorrows. He knew he could do this.

Jovan had just made it to the castle when he had heard the most earth shaking noise of his life. It was like a million men shouted into oblivion all at once. And they had- all the men had began yelling, destroying, ravaging. From somewhere off in the distance, a catapault had thrown a boulder into the side of his town's iconic stone structure. And, Jovan saw, the men had all emerged from the castle with their weapons as the knights of Hawthorne would do.

In the rain and thunder, in the chaos, in all the madness, Jovan was more than confused- how had he not expected Januvia to attack, but all the other soldiers had been prepared, in the castle, waiting for them? Jovan knew sometimes word was slow to get around. But he also knew that they would never want to go and fight without one of their best men.

What was happening to him? Had he lost his credibility as a knight? He was out here, horseless, alone and watching this all from afar. He knew he had to get past them all so that he could go fight from inside the castle. That would be the key to him making it through this. To guard the castle, it must be done from the inside.

If the invaders could be kept from coming in, he would be able to prevent many things from even happening in the first place. If only maybe he could shout out to one of his men, and they would see him and guard the way for him to come inside. But this, he thought, would draw unwanted attention to him as well.

The Januvia soldiers had all swept in on horseback and came in like nightfall would- suddenly, quietly, all at once. They surrounded the castle evenly on all sides and made it impossible for him to get in without being spotted. Jovan knew he would have to make a run for it somehow. He would not be able to overthink- he would have to put it out of his mind and just do it.

Colors and chaos surrounded him. In a different life, he would have known what to do. Now he sat here at the edge of the forest, watching it all. He felt like a total failure. He felt pathetic after he had been such a great soldier-he was at his lowest. There are ways for him to overcome this. He had been smart in the past, able to make it-and now here he was, hopeless and lost.

Hawthorne was fighting back with everything they had. Rain was still drenching the earth, the air was heavy with Summer. There was deafening noise all around him. Everything at this moment had supreme intensity. They were trying to get in and invade the castle, trying to get through all openings and force their way through. Jovan saw their fighting, he saw the pure hate in their eyes- and suddenly, he found himself.

Jovan once again felt a fire ignite inside of him. A warrior, an animalistic innate madness- the madness that swam through his blood, sparking an inferno that lit him up- suddenly, Jovan the warrior was back. Here, out in the middle of the renaissance town, during the storm of the century, surrounded by only his enemies, he knew that he had some fight left in him. In his mind, he was no longer immortal, he was no longer a man. He was a monster, he was a warrior, his golden heart beat for a legend, his strong lungs breathing for an iron soldier.

Jovan charged into the crowd of januvia soldiers. He let out a cry until his lungs could go no longer. To Jovan, it was a stranger yelling, it was not him, it was a barbarian. But it was him, fearless and ready. All he had with him were his arrows. Beneath his clothing he was his naked vulnerable self. But Jovan knew that he would have to show no fear, and hesitate none. His beautiful young eyes showed so much age, so much anger, so much intent. When he ran through the crowd, he put his hands on the men. Most of them were caught off guard. One man, older and with a burly dark beard, jumped upon him.

The man tried to hold him down. He tried to beat him, tried to hold him down. The man's dark eyes seared through him. They were unforgiving. The only thing Jovan had done to him was fight for the other side. Jovan brought up his fists and tried to beat him down. He was able to get on top of the knight. He grabbed his hands and made one swift move for his sword. If Jovan could reach the sword, the lifeline, he would be able to defend himself much easier.

Jovan grabbed the weapon. He leaped up off the ground and made a run for it. He knew he should leave the man be. After taken his weapon from him, he had jeopardized him enough, and decided to leave him to his own devices.

Jovan was so close to being inside. He did not know how exactly he would get in. Jovan would definitely need to have a talk with Torin after this battle- Not being warned of this battle, not being ready, put him in a tough position. He was able to fight off one man with his bare hands, but there were hundreds more still thirsty for Hawthorne blood.

Hawthorne royalty would need to be completely wiped out for them to stop their path of destruction. Unfortunately for them, Hawthorne soldiers were just as resilient.

Jovan ran up to the side of the castle, and made a feeble attempt at climbing the castle wall. He put his foot up and lifted up on a ground window. This may have seemed to be not such a smart move for Jovan- but lucky for him, he was spotted by one of his comrades.

Anaxis was the soldier behind the window. When their eyes met, he froze. "Jovan," he shouted, obviously caught off guard. Jovan gasped for air, as he had been holding his breath the whole time, not sure who he might find behind this window. He was lucky it was a man in his colors.

"Anaxis," Jovan managed, "help me in." Anaxis grabbed Jovan's upper body up and just like he was nothing, help force him in through the window. They found themselves hunkered down for a second beneath the line of fire.

"Sire, we thought you might be sick. We did not know why you had not come to fight with us. But I am glad to see you are here and well. We need your skill in a fight like this." Jovan was just puzzled. He had no idea what was going on. Something must have gone wrong in the line of communication, as Jovan was always the first to line up at every fight.

"Anaxis, why did you think I was sick? I had not heard anything about this fight. I happened upon these men, I was walking out and I ran into their mob, and was stuck outside with no armor and horse."

The look on his comrade's face was stone. The expression was that of a man that had just realized his thoughts were only a tangle of lies. "Jovan, we were told you were wounded at home, and had not been out in days. No one thought you were able to fight."

Jovan felt a pit of raw anger build up in the pit of his stomach. Obviously, someone was sticking their nose where it did not belong.

But now, this was not the time to figure it all out. He had a fight on his hands.

"Anaxis, I promise you, I am ok. I am not sure where this came from. But I always want to be with my men when they need me." "Glad to have you back, Sire," Anaxis offered. Jovan immediately slinked away. He knew the drill for this. He would have to find an expected place to hide near a weak part of the castle. He would need to be hidden but have all eyes on them.

Jovan's untrusting hand stayed on the handle of his stolen sword. He wanted his sparrows, his armor, here to shield his mortal body. Jovan worked his way down a few feet from Anaxis and hunched down below a window. He could stay hidden and shoot his arrows out of the opening.

A thundering, solid, and unmistakable sound came from down the castle corridor. As Jovan looked over his shoulder, he saw something beautiful. It was valorous, it was incredible, it was fearless. It was something only from his time. It was something that made God laugh and cry at the same time.

It was a brigade of Hawthorne knights coming down the hallway, galloping through on horseback. The crowd of horses and men seemed to stop for a minute as they all came through. The stampede stopped for no man, as some had to jump out of the way to avoid being trampled. Though they moved quickly and chaotically through the crowded corridor, Jovan could make out one striking stallion, fully clad in colors and restless in the crowd. Jovan knew he was looking up at his enemy, today his comrade, going forth into the madness.

Jovan did not know why they would have gotten their horses like this, or to what part of the castle they were going. But he did know that each part had to be protected and the horses and men definitely did provide an unworldly sight, the whole lot of them obviously running toward something.

Jovan figured they were going to the top of the castle, the very top where the king was stowed away, and they were all going fully armed to provide the best shield they could for their town. If their king went down, the town would slowly start to unwind and maybe even slowly crumble. The king is what held them together and they came in as the second strongest link. The church was third, and next was just the town and all its people. People like Torin and Gracie. Though, Jovan knew, both of them had a place in this crazy plan-Gracie would marry one of these soldiers and Torin would become one. Jovan prayed for their souls before either of these could happen.

Of course Samuel was leading their pack. He was like a son to the King and nothing would ever get past him. When Samuel was angry, he had a drive that nothing would stand against. Samuel was the kind of person that would shout out in pain and fury then run deeper and face first into it.

Jovan could see some of the chaos going on down below. He was high above them all as he was up in the castle and shooting down at them. Jovan had shot his arrows carefully as he put full focus into every aim. He traced the arrows in the air as the soared, then fell to hit or miss his target. He never lost the feeling he had when he shot at a man.

Even if that man were trying to kill him, Jovan always found it to be a hard act to swallow. Another person's life was not his to take. His heart would beat hard and heavy for them. His mind was always stuck in these moments, storing up memories to later play back in his dreams.

The men kept their enemies from coming on the inside. The fight was brutal. Jovan was having to constantly stay on alert, never to let his guard down and never to let his emotions take over. From his upstairs lookout he could see many men fall and many fight back. Januvia soldiers were relentless.

The battle was pretty much still being fought from the inside, the rain still drove on. The storm would go for as long as the battle. The next time Jovan would see the sun would be days into fighting. On this day, the fighting would be over, the castle grounds would be destroyed, their bodies would be pushed past their limit. The sun would shine boldly and dauntingly upon them, reminding them that life must go on.

What now? He thought, as Jovan had lived another day, and he was now supposed to pick himself back up and go back to his life as he knew it. Was he living his life to fight battles, while never winning the fights he had within?

Blood from men and blood from horses washed down deep into the earth as the rain continued to torture them. War overtook them for the time being. At this time, nothing ran their lives like the fight they refused to let tear them down. The men that had been fighting above him on the upper layer had held their ground and not let anyone get through. Jovan could see arrows raining down from up above him. He knew they were sending them down at their enemies as they looked down from above. They had fought relentlessly and tirelessly to protect their hallowed ground.

Jovan had been fighting for two days straight at this point. He found himself now at the castle's entrance. Januvia soldiers had been trying to break down this door, they had gotten a battering ram to crash into it repeatedly, attempting to get through and ambush. He and a few of his other men were behind the door and guarding it. They stood using their bodies as human shields. Knights were like that- they would die before being dishonored. Jovan had been in the front of the group and had taken the lead on this group of fighters. "Hold your ground!" Jovan yelled through gritted teeth. His muscles were strained, he knew his men had expended all their energy and they were tired- tired of fighting, tired of war, tired of being tired. But here they all were, using all they had to keep Januvia from what they were trying to do most- get inside and rip them apart.

"Keep holding, don't give in!" Jovan was a born leader- he was forceful and passionate and people listened to him. His presence was a blessing for his troop. He stepped up when he saw their tired eyes and their broken spirits. Jovan's spirit would never be broken- but it had been tried. "We are holding them back!" One of the men yelled, in response and frustration. The strength of ten valorous men was also giving Januvia a run for their money, as they had tried every option and were beginning to give out themselves. The soldiers gave up trying to bust through. Jovan collapsed in the floor, perhaps from exhaustion, perhaps from not knowing where to go from here, and he looked all around him. He could see his men scattered through the castle, up against the wall and posing by windows.

He wondered what she was doing right now. Was she thinking of Samuel, and worried for him, as he was fighting this war? Was she thinking about him? Was she worried for him too? Was she thinking that the two men she loved may never return, or that they might and she would have to give one of them up?

To love was to put yourself through hell. To love was to not know. Love was torture, but it was also not thinking about these things- because the person on your mind was worth it, and doing anything for them was more intense than any kind of pain this life could offer. Jovan would fight and push through, because he knew that there was someone that he wanted to see again.

He would be her soldier, and fight for her the rest of his life, no matter what, forever.

Jovan had left this world for a minute. His mind and his muscles were exhausted. He prayed to his maker for the storm and the war to go away, and for brighter days to come. He knew that Januvia was going in for a second try at the door as he saw it shutter, as it was being hit from the outside. A sturdy frame was no match for a group of angry men. Jovan's arms and legs were numb, his heart was still fighting. The anger he got from Januvia's relentlessness started a fire inside of him. And now, after fighting two days straight with no food, water, or sleep, he let out a battle cry to be heard across the kingdom, and he ran with strength that he did not know he had. Jovan ran toward the door, yelling as he went: "men, we have to stop them!"

And what he did next could either be brave or foolish.

Jovan ran straight toward the castle door and pushed it open and ran right into the crowd of men that he had been fighting for so long. But, because the men always looked out for one another, a group of others followed him. And they faced those that had threatened them most as they all went straight in with their swords ready, and their fates in God's hands.

Jovan was beat down a few times and he just kept finding the strength to get back up. This was the way that Hawthorne beat Januvia. When the men began to join the fight outside, they started to wear down the Januvia soldiers at an alarming rate. The knights that had come inside on horseback even came out to join them. These were the men that finished what Jovan and his followers had started.

Soon, Jovan got his wish. This was the second day of battle and this was also the last day. Jovan dropped to his knees as he saw the sun break through the stone sky. There was hope now, the bad times were over. He looked to the sky and thanked God for his blessings. There was a sun, there was a new day, and there were new days ahead. There were chances for him now. Since the fighting was over, days of glory was all he could hope for.

But now, the hardest part was to move on. The exhaustion, the hopelessness, the brutality- it was all over, and Hawthorne had pulled through. Only men like this could have stood up to these bloodthirsty fighters. Jovan did feel proud, he knew he was definitely special in all the ways he needed to be. He knew that his people would find honor in it, and praise him. But he knew that this was not all about honor.

If Jovan were to think about it, he would see he was fighting another man's fight. The fight between Hawthorne and Januvia was nothing he had done, nothing he had started- but yet here he was, his heart now pounding and his lungs breathing in and out, catching up to all the energy he had exerted, as he looked across this battlefield. It was scary because it was right in the middle of his own town and now those that did not make it lay mangled and lifeless just feet away from him.

Why had God always chose him to come through? Was there still a plan, a purpose for him? Jovan felt so much like giving up. But he knew now was the time for healing. The town would have to take their fallen soldiers and have a burial for them, and peace would hopefully be restored. This was usually the quiet time for the kingdom. Those that had not been involved never did see the damage until it was over. When a man did not come home, everyone would know- the fault was all on his love affair with knighthood.

Knighthood was only one of Jovan's toxic affairs. It seemed that no matter what he did, he was playing with fire. Everything seemed to be dangerous to him. Yet the adrenaline and the insanity of it all kept him coming back for more. And now that this battle was over, he had a few personal things he would need to take care of. Jovan knew someone had been prying into his personal life, as the lie that was told about him being sick was not true. It had been a lie that could have gotten him seriously injured as well. He would need to trace it back and find the source.

Jovan's mind went to Torin. His adolescent, awkward, and hardworking apprentice was one of the only people that communicated between he and the other knights. But Torin had always been reliable and had never lied before. Jovan got a knot in his throat as he got a bad feeling about this- he may never find out, but if things like this kept happening, he could lose his credibility as a knight for good.

Jovan found himself sitting in the mud as the people around him stirred around chaotically, seeing if any of their soldiers had been killed along the way. He gazed at the sword he had used this entire time- the one he had stolen from the Januvia knight. The sword had slain its carrier and had been used at the hands of the enemy, as Jovan relied on it the duration of the battle. As he tilted the blade in the sun, he could notice a faint design in the metal as it gleamed gallantly. Jovan ran the sword along his pants in order to get the blood and dirt off and this revealed a roaring lion, jumping after its prey. He studied the design as it was elegant and elaborate. This must be what happens, he thought, when a sparrow and a lion fight.

Jovan shoved the sword down into the mud and picked himself up. Hawthorne had lost only three men, as Januvia had lost nearly a third of theirs. Fighting from inside had given them the advantage for sure. Jovan was always grateful each time he walked away from a fight.

The soldiers who had their horses trotted around the massacre. "We can't find Samuel," one of them yelled desperately, "Has anyone seen Samuel?" Jovan was silent and his blood ran cold. Could someone have possibly overpowered him? Jovan was frozen as he saw them gallop away into the woods, splitting up, thinking that maybe there would be signs of him there.

Anaxis approached Jovan. "Anaxis, thank you, so much for helping me back there," Jovan said immediately, "I might not would have made it without you." Jovan extended his hand for a handshake, but Anaxis pulled him in for a half-hug instead. "Jovan you would have made it. You would have." His words were determined and bold and meant to be stamped onto Jovan's conscience, as sometimes your mind was your worst enemy.

"I'm so glad you made it out alive. Maybe they will not try to fight us anymore," Anaxis said. Jovan knew they could only hope. "I can't wait to get something to eat," he laughed, "and rest up some. If they give us time for rest, I know we will be strong again." Jovan had been strong and he was strong even now, but he did not know how much longer he could be this way. He was a good-hearted man with a tainted soul. He knew the other soldiers were this way as well, it was obvious in their eyes.

Jovan's youth had been taken by his lifestyle, his humanity by the consequences of it. "The burials will be the most difficult," he replied to his comrade, and stalked away to join the search for the only brother that he could never see eye-to-eye with. He did not know if Samuel would even respond to him, but he figured if nothing else, it was because he was a fellow knight. Jovan headed to the woods as he spotted a rider on a white horse coming up from the distance. The rider was young, black hair and, as he got closer, Jovan could see his ice blue stare. It was Torin.

Torin was sixteen and Jovan was twenty five that summer. They were both young, but in very different ways. Torin was young in the ways of the world. He was green like the grass that covered the earth in spring. His immature follies were a product of his fumble to adulthood, a forgiving reminder that he would move on from them soon. His youth was just that kind- the kind he would outgrow, the kind he would move on from. Torin would admire girls from afar and quickly stumble away from them.

Jovan's youth was very much alive in his heart. He was at a prime in his life. He was fit and able, but he was much older and wiser in his ways. He knew how to handle the hard things. He knew that life could sometimes throw punches that you could not recover from. It was all about your reaction to the situation. He was the type of young that would romance many girls, and only run from his feelings. He was the type of young that made big mistakes, that would stay out drinking, and stumble in the next day as he accepted his honor and praise, asking God for forgiveness.

Torin jumped down off the horse. "Sire, I came as fast as I could. I wanted to help anyone that might have gotten hurt, and see if you were okay," he stammered. Jovan looked down at Torin. His six-foot-something was no match for Torin's average five and a half. "Torin, we need to go into the woods," he breathed, "Samuel is missing. We need to see if he is still okay."

Samuel could have even gotten kidnapped- Januvia could have

taken him, as he was engaged to their king's daughter, and they might be holding him for ransom. Jovan knew that crazier things had happened.

As Torin got back on his horse and began to ride away, Jovan stopped him. "Torin," he started in a serious tone, "I hope you know that lying to the kingdom is serious." Torin's look shifted into one that was baffled, and he stopped for a second. "Jovan, what do you mean? I have not lied to anyone. What is this about?" Jovan felt instant regret, as he already knew it had not been Torin to make up the lie. "When the battle broke out, I was not waiting with the other soldiers because no one gave me word they were coming. Someone had said that I should not be alerted because I was too sick to be fighting." Torin nodded. "Oh yes," he started, "River came to me and told me you were unfit to fight. That was why I did not come by and warn you."

As Torin galloped away, Jovan felt an uncontrollable pent up anger inside of him. He fell completely backwards into the mud and looked straight up to the sky. Had she been trying to get him killed or make him look bad? She had no business interfering with something as serious as war.

And as Jovan lay there, he looked up into the forest canopy that shielded him from the harsh sun. Suddenly, a flock of sparrows flew from the tallest tree. Jovan, though mangled here in the grass, laughed.

Sparrows. The birds he wore for protection had just flown away from him.

Chapter 5

Jovan would now face the other depths of his complicated existence. He would go back and face River and her dark selfish soul, he would face the girl that was his greatest weakness and strength at the same time. He would also face the people of his town and smile and wave to them and know that when he would sleep at night, his thoughts would go back to times of despair.

Rebuilding himself and remembering his purpose would keep him going. People like Gracie would keep him going. The feeling he got when he felt his blood pulsing beneath his skin, when he would smile over the simple things, and the feeling of riding high and fierce into all things forbidden were the things he lived for. Today, he knew, he would make it. He would get through these things and not let them push him over the edge.

But finding out what River was up to would be the greatest challenge. She was a woman with many layers. She was beautiful but bad and she would stop at nothing to get what she wanted.

"Jovan," a voice rang over him, he had been staring at the birds for so long. A face appeared in place of the birds above him. Torin had returned, and was gazing down at his superior.

"Why are you laying in the mud? Are you okay?" Jovan suddenly realized that he had been lying useless on the ground when he should have been searching with everyone else. "I had to get my bearings," Jovan said after a second of hesitation. "You did not have to come back for me. I'm fine." Jovan got up and dusted himself off, and began walking in the direction of the search party. At least he could do his greatest service for now, he thought. Patching up the past would be taken care of later.

"Are you sure?" Torin continued to stare at him, uneasy, as he saw his normally composed leader slowly going out of his mind. Jovan tried to be grounded on the surface but a million things were making him crazy, testosterone driving him and overriding his thoughts.

"Torin, I need you to go into the woods, now, to go look for Samuel, don't waste any more time!" Jovan's patience was exhausted and he had too much to deal with right now. Jovan ran his hand through his now growing-out hair, a dirty blonde mess tangled with sweat, blood, and dirt. The hair fell back down over one eye, and as he tried to brush it away, it fell right back in front of his line of vision.

Torin turned to head into the forest. He would never question his leader, and he would do his best to be courageous, just as he was expected to be.

Jovan stalked on into the forest. The woods were calm. The now beaming sun casted a ghostly glow over the quiet and still landscape. The other soldiers that had headed in before him were long gone now, probably miles deep into the trees, and it was as if they had never even been there in the first place.

It was just him. Right now, Jovan knew he was solitary in his surroundings. The glow from sun beams welcomed him back to life as the past few days had been dark. He found solace within himself now. Everything he really needed was right here. For the millionth time he wished he could stay here and never have to face anyone again, and live out his days with peace in his heart.

But now, the other knights needed him. And he was valorous, and brave, and strong, so he set forth on into the woods, not knowing what to expect.

Jovan heard rustling in the bushes behind him. Taken aback, he got his bow and arrows ready, expecting an attack. But instead a beautiful copper stallion ran from the trees, obviously startled. The horse was clad in crimson red and gold. This was Samuel's horse.

The horse ran quickly in the other direction. It seemed to be escaping from something as it ran chaotically away from whatever was taunting it. To see Samuel's horse without him, galloping desperately away was a bad sign. Jovan felt a surge of dread go throughout his body. He hesitantly stepped through the brush up ahead of him. If he kept going, he would come out to the brook, and a nice clearing in the forest. Maybe, he thought, he could find some signs of him there.

The woods were still and all but dead. They were anticipating him, they continued to draw him in even further. Jovan slowly ambled toward the meadow in his trance-like state. He could see a shimmer of light from the ground. Something shiny on the ground was gleaming from the sun. The glimmer caught his eye and he walked toward the object.

As he got closer, Jovan could see that the object was large, and made of metal. He walked even closer. His heart sank, his blood ran cold. Jovan felt as if he were paralyzed, because he could suddenly feel nothing. Breathing was hard for him when there was numbness throughout his body. He thought maybe that he would vomit, but since he had not eaten in days, there was nothing that would come up. A sick, morbid feeling was all he knew right now- everything else no longer existed.

Samuel and Jovan both remained part of the earth- but Samuel's soul had long since left this place. Jovan knew this as he saw the metal was a suit of armor, and he flipped the body over to see a soulless and lifeless face of his enemy. A large rock lay beside him, covered with blood, and Jovan knew that Samuel had not been killed in the fight- an enemy had found him and attacked him in the forest, beating him to death with this rock.

Samuel still clung to his sword. Armored hands had raised it but were not swift enough, as the enemy had ambushed him, and unleashed their attack. Jovan silently panicked in his mind for a moment. A thousand thoughts ran through his mind. It seemed to have been a brutal attack.

Jovan's panic caused him to step away. He knew he should do something- he should alert the others, he should try to get Samuel out of here, and he should stay on guard- in case he was next.

Jovan wondered when it would all end. Had there not been enough damage done already? Samuel would have rolled his eyes at Jovan, he would have told him to go away- but right now, Samuel had faded away and nothing would ever change it. Jovan ran to find the others.

They had overlooked him as they headed deeper and deeper into the forest, and he knew they were probably at the beach by now. But because Jovan had seen the horse, he knew that Samuel had to be nearby. Jovan did not want to leave his comrade, but he decided it best to go find the others and alert them.

Jovan stumbled through the woods, his mind was hazy and his thoughts unclear. He could no longer think clearly. Dark thoughts and bad auras filled the air around him. He felt that no matter how fast he ran, he would not reach them fast enough. No matter how many times he had seen death, no matter how many gallons of blood had been spilled in his kingdom at his hand, nothing would take away the feeling he had now. Jovan's stomach had twisted up into painful knots. He was desperate to find his comrades. Seeing them and feeling a sense of togetherness would help to ease some of his pain.

He did not want to shout for them. This would draw attention to himself, and if there were still enemies out there, he could be next. Samuel had been one of the king's most valiant and skilled soldiers. He was a fearless man. Samuel was known for the attitude he had of being fearless. He would be the first to run right into enemy lines. He was never afraid of being hurt or being killed, because he knew he was equipped to fight.

Jovan was the same way. He was also among some of the kingdom's finest- he was a leader, and he was skilled with archery and other weapons. He could think fast and move faster. His brain would tire but he would still come back with answers- they were a lot alike, actually.

Jovan pondered that maybe this was why he and Samuel never got along. To have such equal skill and power was such a rare thing.

Yet, both men had just that. Samuel may have been trying to prove himself, Jovan thought, and maybe Jovan had been his greatest threat.

But now even that would not matter. Jovan saw Samuel's blood and saw his armor, and that they wore the same colors. He could no longer picture Samuel as his enemy. He saw him only as a human being now, as death had claimed yet another victim.

Had Januvia slain Samuel because of his skill? Were they trying to pick off the best knights, one by one? Was Jovan next? Was Januvia even the culprit in this case?

Jovan was sweating all over, the thin shirt he had saturated with his panicked response to this situation. The summer heat added to it. He could see a group of his men up ahead, and as he ran to them, they turned to see him there.

"Samuel," was all Jovan could say, breathing hard and still in his state of shock. He knew the truth would hurt. He knew that when he would tell them, they would have to see for themselves. "Jovan, what is it? Are you hurt?" Benedict interrogated, obviously knowing that something was wrong. "Samuel is dead in the meadow." He said it all at once to get it overwith. The faces of his men dropped as they processed the news.

"Sire, are you sure it was him?" Benedict asked. Jovan shook his head violently. "Yes, yes, I saw his horse and his armor – and his face, the life was beaten out of him."

The men galloped toward the meadow in pursuit of what Jovan had said. To be a knight, he knew, was to see death and know death very well. It was almost like a forbidden acquaintance. But for some unknown reason, the death of Samuel had shaken him up inside.

When death would come to a man, she would look so beautiful. Death was a beautiful mistress clad in a black lace veil, that would come to a person in distress, and quiet their screams. She would take them up in her arms and she would tell them to come with her, to join her world. It was a dark world, but peaceful, and it would take them away from the pain they felt on earth. Some would follow and some would not. But all of them could tell you how chilling it was to have death run her hand along your face, look you in the eye and offer her hand. Those that took it would never be part of this life again.

Jovan imagined that Samuel had been taken out too quickly to have much time to spend with the angel of death. She had taken him without hesitation. Whatever had happened to him had been so brutal that he had gone with her in order to get away from it. And Jovan knew that knights were not easy to take.

The body was lying in the same place as he had left it when they returned. Jovan helped the men put his body on one of the men's horse. Together they all rode back in silence. To have Samuel and his dark presence around was something they had gotten used to for the past six years as Samuel had been a knight. His short-lived career had been a great attribution to their army.

For six years Jovan had fought beside him. Jovan had misunderstood him, and he had competed with him. Though Samuel may have had a black heart, Jovan could not help but shutter when he looked at him, and feel sadness for his loss of life.

Returning home from the battle was like picking up all the pieces and putting himself back together again. Each time he came back from a fight, the pieces were always different. He would always lose a few of them from himself. He would gain pieces to replace the ones he had lost- they would be pieces of pain, of fearlessness, of another chip on his shoulder. Each time he would come back a different man. He knew that, no matter what he had been through, he would have to move on somehow. He would get a little stronger each time.

Gracie had been all of his missing pieces. Up until now, he never realized how much he would need another person. Now after coming home with days of no sleep or food, the only thing he wanted was to see her again. She did not know that her betrothed was passed away. She did not know that she would never see him again- someone she had planned her life with. Jovan had a sinking feeling, as he knew that she would most certainly be distraught.

But she had been the first person he thought about when he came back to his quiet house in the woods. He knew that in order to feel ok again, he would need to see her, and they could then mourn together.

His house was quiet and unbothered like nothing had ever happened, it had been a quiet place awaiting his return. And now, as he walked through the door of his home, the feeling of loneliness hit him hard. He honestly did not know where he would go from here.

Jovan lay in his bed that night, somehow unable to find sleep even after a long day of rebuilding the town and helping the hurt soldiers. If anything rang true in his heart, it was loyalty. He would always be loyal to his men. Jovan would always uphold his honor and he would do anything to stand with his fellow soldiers. For him, it was the greatest honor he could have in his life. The loyalty of a knight was unlike any other. It was the best of any.

Why was he the way that he was? How much had knighthood really shaped his life? Would he have been the same person without it? Would his heart have been so tortured, his mind so brilliant? Would his thoughts be so darkened and his pride be fulfilled, would he find himself gaining glory from other things? Or would he be a part of the crowd, just like everyone else, a person that longed for the things he had now?

He would never know what it would be like to be that way, to see things from the other side. And he did not understand why it was so hard to figure out why things were the way that they were. He felt God should have given this life to someone better, someone wiser, and someone more secure with their life.

Sleep could not find him, dreams could not fulfill him. All that he could find was the darkness that shrouded him. The quiet around him was a sanctuary, as silence had evaded him the past few days. He knew it was a rare treasure. Before, he would have gone out to the town and wander, to soothe his restless muscles and his invading thoughts. But now, he dared not leave his bed and the lonely corner of his shadowed room.

He found many of his thoughts going back to her. Gracie's forget-me-not smile, a sugar coated kiss and sapphire eyes. Many things had enamored him during his lifetime, but none exactly like she had. Her skin had been warm like summer and her laugh was a melody he would play over and over in the soundtrack of his mind.

If she had been a month, she would have been October. A thousand different colors shone through the image he had of her; her lips were the inside of a rose, red and timeless. Her cheeks were pink dogwood blossom. Her hair was auburn like the sunsets and azure eyes like the skies. Her touch would give him chills, as would October wind, and her presence warm and longing, as are the last days of Summer before fading into fall.

But now, July heat came in through his window and he perspired under his blanket. Long days would turn into long nights, and the cycle would continue. He would have to go make things right with a number of people. He wanted to visit Gracie. He wanted to confront River- and he wanted to talk with his men, after the war, to be sure they would all be okay.

But it would always be ok. No matter what, somehow and in some way, they were always okay.

After he lay in bed after another sleepless night, Jovan rose early the next morning. Sunrise flooded through his window. Warm heat rays were already slipping in. He got up quickly and began to get dressed. He knew where he would go-he would go to town and wait by the fruit stand, where he knew she would come to buy fruit, as she did each morning.

Maybe now was not the time. Maybe after the death of her high society fiancé was not the best time to approach her, but he did not want her to feel as alone as he did, because he had decided that loneliness was the worst pain that could ever exist.

A beautiful day followed the tragedies that had occurred the day before. Walking to town was more of a chore than he had anticipated. He was sore in his joints and In his muscles. His stomach ached from hunger. He needed to eat very soon. Though much of the town was still destroyed, merchants still took to their usual posts, with supplies ready to sell to the demanding townspeople.

He approached the fruit stand and began to smile, as the sight of it reminded him that he may get to see her soon. The merchant behind the stand seemed to notice, as she looked up and met his gaze.

"Sire Jovan!" She swooned, surprised to see him here. "So nice to see you here, and in such good spirits!" Jovan suddenly felt foolish, as this was not a time for joy. "Well thank you, I am just glad to have fought the battle and won. And to have made it through." The merchant nodded, she was an elderly woman, aged from field working and adversity.

"Yes, sire, as we know that you all do such a great job fighting for us all in the town." Jovan was silent for a moment. "I do my best," he finally replied, "as we all do." Jovan gazed at all the fruit she had available, so many different things that may not be found otherwise. There were apples, oranges, bananas, grapes, kiwi, strawberries, blueberries, pears, raspberries, blackberries, and more. His hunger overtook him at that moment. "I would like to purchase some of your goods," he offered. "I have not eaten in days." He winked at the lady, to try and lighten the mood, but she began throwing an assortment of fruit into a bag, and held it out to him. "For my warrior, please take it," she offered, "No charge at all!" Jovan hesitantly took the bag. After a second, he reached in his pocket to take out some money, and he put it in the woman's hand, closing her hand up around it. Her face dropped as she saw the generous gift.

"Thank you, but I really do insist that you take it," he said. She put the money in her pocket and thanked him back. "Can you do something else for me?" he asked. She looked back up at him and smiled. "Of course Sire," she replied. "There is a girl. She comes here each day and buys your fruit. I need to see her. She has dark blonde hair and puts the fruit in a basket. Will you give her the message to meet me by the creek?"

And then Jovan went down to the water. He found a shady spot and sat down in dewy grass with his bag of fruit. He would not leave here until he could see her. He did not want to go back to his house as the same man he was now. He wanted to return with a picture of her smile in his mind, and the feeling she gave him that radiated throughout his existence. Maybe that would change things, he thought. Maybe when it happened, he would be reminded all over again of why he was out here in the first place.

A daydream, he imagined, was just that; something that would come to you during waking hours, something that would come along in thought or in person and change the course of the day, something beautiful to fill the void of a usually darkened world. Something to give you hope and make you imagine, something to help you disappear into a place that was neither here nor there, but a place that was your own that only you can understand. And when she would come to him, it would be like all his dreams come true.

His own true reality was his day dream-because he could reach out and touch her, he could take her in, and he could get lost in a prism that she created with her velvet words and everlasting love.

The merchant had given him so many kinds of fruit- there was an orange, a few apples, grapes and a pear. He started to peel the orange, fleshy peeling rolling up as he stripped it of its outer layer. The juice dripped down his chin as his ravenous nature took over, as he had not eaten in two days. It was like God's candy, a blessing to grace his lips and parched, tortured tongue.

And as he began to bite into an apple, the forbidden fruit, his forbidden love could be seen approaching him. A summer haze surrounded her. She too held a basket of fruit and she swung it back and forth, like a pendulum, as she walked. Her look was somber. Her gaze was down and her hair fell down over one eye. Nothing would describe her better than knowing she had had a true love lost.

"Jovan!" She perked up a little as she saw him, still sitting under his tree. He stood up to greet her. "I thought it must be you, the fruit lady just told me that a knight was waiting here." "I am your knight," he said quickly. But he must not forget what had happened- the one she had planned a life with was now dead, under the ground and here he was above it, and still living the lie he had had before this had all happened.

He tried to convince himself that he was not wrong, that the fire lit up inside of him was not out of accident. "I bet you have heard the news," He said now in a more relaxed manner, a serious tone in his shaking voice. Gracie pulled away from him, and covered her face as she began to cry. Her tears were raindrops from the Heavens, a lightning storm in her typically sunny forecast. There was definitely a storm brewing inside her.

Jovan went in to grab her and bring her close. He was not one for emotion. He was not one to hold someone as they would cry. But his heart ached now, for he had seen it with his own eyes, an image that he would never shake- his comrade face down, as his suit of armor had failed him, and his men had done the same.

"He was my brother in arms," He started, tightening his grip. Right now, they were neither friends nor lovers; they were two tortured souls, shaken by the loss of a misunderstood man, which made sense to neither of them. "And a great knight. You were lucky to have known him." Jovan felt a tear fall from his Juniper eyes. Samuel was frozen in time now, he would never be a day older, and he would forever leave his mark on Hawthorne.

"I feel lost now," Gracie replied. "I was going to marry him. Now I have no direction in life. But you, Jovan, have been the only sane thing." Jovan let her pull away, as she tried to dry her eyes. "And now, I guess, I will have to return to Januvia. My father will find someone else for me." Jovan's heart dropped. He was selfish, maybe, to be thinking of himself. "Gracie, you don't have to leave. Spend a little more time with me."

Just a little time- a day, a week, a month. No matter what, it would never be enough. His clock would start the countdown and he would never be satisfied. Their love had never been allowed in the first place- it was both the worst and best thing he had ever done. "Come away with me again, let me help you forget."

A drug was in his system that made him think senseless thoughts, and the drug was love, he thought. He no longer cared what would happen to him. He did not care what it would take or what price he would pay. He wanted to be with her- but he knew it could never happen.

She took his outstretched hand. Her body trembled. "Just let me be your bad decision," he begged. "One more night, come and get lost with me." Gracie smiled a somber smile at him. She let him take her hand, and holding their fruit, they started walking again toward the beach.

Jovan remembered their last night at the beach- everything was beautiful then and everything was the same. The battle with Januvia had not yet happened, his life was confusing, but he knew that he would figure it out somehow. Now he was not so sure. He had had so much guilt for being with her, but so much pleasure at the same time. Now here he was, going back, and it felt so good just like the first time.

The first time feeling was a thing that he would never feel again or with anyone else. It was something he did because it was summer time, because he was young, because it was night, because he had no one telling him no- and because her forbidden desire was not allowed. This time it was fueled by desire and ecstasy, and searching for what would happen when he was not alone.

They walked together through the woods, down the trail and past the meadow- where everything had happened. Jovan knew an ocean was waiting for them.

Gracie had been mostly silent. She had held to him tightly, and he wanted her to know he would hang on as long as she would. She began to stare into his gaze. A comfort passed over him, and he knew that everything would be ok, and that they would always have one another.

"Gracie I never want you to leave," he started. "If you leave, I will have nobody. And you are my strength right now." She had been his high during the low points. "When I was fighting, I thought about you, and that I needed to make it, so that I would see you again." He was too pushy, he thought; maybe, she was not ready to be that serious with him.

"I thought about you too Jovan," She said apprehensively. "I wondered if I would see you again. But now, I have to figure out what comes next." She stopped for a minute, thinking. "I want to start over somewhere new. But the past kings of my hometown have made it hard for me to be accepted anywhere else- everybody thinks we are violent people."

"You want to leave?" Jovan, shocked, asked. His heart dropped once again- what was this for? What was the meaning of all he had done? He had tried hard to fight for her, and yet she still wanted to leave him.

She was the type of girl to marry the sons of kings, the legends of a town- to always be taken care of, to be treasured by men all over. He had not seen this until now.

Jovan, though legendary, was mild mannered and obedient- he was not a risk, he was not exciting. His only vice was the thing that gave him all his strength- knighthood. And now it was her, sitting and staring into him with eyes that matched the ocean water- and telling him that she would leave soon.

"This town has nothing for me. You are here- but we can never be together now, Jovan. And if I stay here, I will be leaving my family. This hiding out is something that will never work. And we can't hide forever."

Jovan knew it was true- if they were to be together, it would be too obvious- and too soon after Samuel. He could never show his dishonor in such a way. How long could they hide from the world exactly? The only ones to know about their affair was God above and the sun, moon, and stars that had looked down upon them.

"What comes next is finding ourselves," Jovan answered, "and living true to ourselves. I understand if you think you have to leave Gracie, but I ask that you think about it for a little longer before you do-think about all we've had, and how easy it all has been, and how fast all of it happened. Nothing will ever measure up to that."

She put her head down, because she knew it was true. They both knew deep down it was true. But their steamy affair had led them to dark places in their souls. It had given them guilt like never before. It had made Jovan crazy, like a rabid dog after his meat, after he had gotten to be with her- because now nothing else mattered to him. He did not know his old self anymore, because those things no longer existed to him. Gracie had meant the world to him, and now she was leaving.

He could not leave like she could, and he envied her for that. He could not walk away from his world of knighthood and kingship and pageantry; it was his entire life. It was what made him who he was, and he had nothing else, no other identity than the soldier everyone knew him to be.

He could not blame her, because she was just passing through. She was a dandelion floating on the breeze during a spring day. She would come through and charm those she touched but she would not be here for long. Because angels, he knew, had to go back where they came from eventually. "Just know, that no matter what happens, I will never forget the time we had together. Nothing else was ever like the way I felt with you," she assured him. He knew that she had been a lover, out to find what her heart so desired, and so was he, and so they had found one another, and they had made all the love they needed for a lifetime. But Jovan wanted to do it again.

"Did you love him?" He asked. She gazed through him for a second, thinking. "Yes," she replied, "it was a war within my heart. Because I love you too. But I loved you both differently. I loved you with a passionate love, a love that will live on through time and a love that changed me. I loved Samuel like an obedient wife, like a woman should love her husband. Samuel was stable and safe. But you were so dangerous and alive, and awakened an inner part of me that I've never felt before. And I thank you so much for that."

Jovan was not sure if both types of love were equal- he had only felt what he had had toward her, which had been so real to him.

He could see in her eyes, though, that she was not lying- the look she gave was full of pain and uncertainty. Jovan felt the same- he knew he needed to say goodbye to her and leave her as a thing of his past; a thing that he could remember once in awhile, that he would share only with her, and that would affect him in a way that would make him stop and think awhile, but he would easily forget after a second and move on.

He wanted to be able to move on.

"You are the only girl I have ever loved," Jovan started, "And I don't regret anything that happened between us. And just know that if you ever come back to Hawthorne, I want to see you again." The chase would never end, he knew, the flame would never turn to ash.

Gracie smiled at Jovan, a genuine and loving smile, a smile that warmed him up throughout his insides. He knew suddenly that everything would be ok, that he would move on, that she would find peace somewhere away from here but he would always be in her heart. She would go back to her hometown where he would not fight for her. He would no longer be her knight; he would be the knight that now fought against the ones protecting her.

She grabbed his shirt and pulled him in. Her lips met his, and he melted all over. When he kissed her, he was weak. Weakness was foreign to him but he was aching for more. Weakness could show him another side to himself; he would see everything differently, and have a chance to let other things in.

But they had only kissed for a short minute, and she pulled away from him. "Jovan, for us to be together would be toxic," she breathed. Jovan nodded. To know she thought of them as toxic was disheartening.

"It's time to go," she added. She stood before him. There had been sand in between his toes and wind was combing through his blonde hair. She walked a few steps before he got up. He sat there to ponder, to wonder why, to try and understand why some people only pass through. He wondered why he had met someone he had loved so much and she had slipped right through his fingers.

She was being selfish, maybe; she was thinking of herself to be leaving like she was. But, he thought, maybe he was also being selfish.

He then realized that he not had things figured out after all. He would have to also figure out where to go from here. As he looked to the ocean, he could find no answers. The ocean was desperately fierce. Waves crashed and the water was furious. The water was unsettled and the sunset teased the ocean, calmly surfacing above it.

He and the ocean were both the same. They were both God's troubled creations, they were both full of anger and full of passion. Jovan looked behind him as Gracie was walking away, making her way back to the town and then wherever life would lead her. Jovan stood to follow her. He could feel the life drain from his body. All he had fought for was walking away from him.

Chapter 6

Jovan was left to his own devices- he was just a shell of a man now. His heart had been torn out of him and left on the beach that day. All affinities he had had for her, all the affinity he had left in his body, felt lost to him.

He knew pain was no match for him. He knew how to pick himself back up again and keep going. He had seen death a million times- but for some reason, this was not an image or a feeling he could shake- Samuel's armored body face down in the meadow, Gracie walking away from him.

Jovan had made his way home that night and found himself in a great deal of pain. He had discovered a bottle of liquor locked away in his cabinet. He had went on a walk that night.

This, he knew, was just how everything had started- his drunken self trying hard to put one foot in front of the other. His vision was blurry and his thoughts were racing. They did not make sense, and they all ran together, and, worst of all, they haunted him.

Sparrows had not saved him. Arrows had only protected him from being weak. Castle walls had separated him from a deathly demise. He was no greater than any other being on this earth; he was weak, he knew, he had been weak and foolish for so many things.

He had had an affair. And now, the man he had betrayed was a dead man, a man that wanted to destroy him. The blackness of his drunken night had made his sin so real. Birds did not fly from trees at this time of night, men did not walk the streets. Horses and cattle seldom grazed. So there he had been, holding white knuckled to his bottle of regrets, and wishing things could have been different.

Blood was to blame. The noble blood that pulsed through his veins and kept him alive had been the reason that he was here. This was the dream life- but a nightmare to anyone who lived it. Had he been someone else, maybe Gracie would have always been his. But, he knew, that she belonged to no one. She was a free spirit and wandering soul that could go and come as she would please.

And Jovan was tied down. He was married to knighthood. A cold sweat covered Jovan's body, though it must have been at least ninety degrees. The Summer air had teased him, allowing him to breathe it in and use it up, but then torturing him as he pleaded for relief, pleaded for a way to escape the heat.

By now, he had staggered all the way through his town. He saw the skeletons of booths at night, vacant and patiently awaiting their merchants to return the next morning. He saw the castle's outline in the chalky clouds. The castle, though beaten down, still stood tall as a beacon of strength after the war. The parts that had been destroyed had quickly been rebuilt.

He wondered what it would be like to climb to the tallest balcony and look down each night, the only thing above you being the stars. The town would be yours. The soldiers would defend you- and you would spend your lifetime in a stone mansion, built up to the sky, for the world to see and for you to live in luxury. So much mystery and romance surrounded the palace and so much wonder would be gained.

A privileged life, beautiful clothes, white horses and balls, servants, trumpets, and courtyards- nobility was so glamorous on the surface. But when one lived their life in it, they would see the scandal, the bloodshed, the disgrace to humanity. The nobles thought highly of themselves and wanted everyone else to do the same. They had the final say in this town.

Wind had danced like a ghost through the skeletal trees. Jovan's drunken mind would have fought off any ghost. Because even though he was out in the woods alone at night, he was not afraid of anything.

He would never be afraid. No matter what came at him, he would never run and hide from it. Arrows falling from the sky or a man with dead eyes could never make him think twice.

He smelled of rancid and strong liquor. The smell burned through his nose and he choked as he took another drink. Coughing violently, Jovan collapsed, and would not wake up until sunrise.

The next morning, Jovan awakened in the meadow. Grass stuck to his sweat-drenched skin. He was filthy. Dirt caked under his nails, body odor and the stench of liquor overpowered him. Jovan looked around for a second, disoriented. His head pounded like it might bust open any second now. He wondered if he had been walking through a dream and that he would wake up again and find himself in bed, because he was in denial of the mistake he had made.

This was not the picturesque image everyone had of him. A few feet away, Jovan had vomited. He gagged at the sight of it. Disgusted with himself, he headed toward the water to wash off.

Jovan became naked and waded into the creek. The water was so cold to him, but it was the best thing he had felt in awhile. He watched as days of dirt washed from him and into the clear water. The water was quartz, fish swimming were visible beneath the surface. Jovan held his nose and went under the water. He stopped for a second, holding his breath in underwater solace. He could hear the water trickling past and the dense sounds of underwater movements. Everything seemed to be in slow motion.

As Jovan came up from the water, he squeezed the droplets out of his hair and brushed the now ear-length hair out of his eyes. He was rugged and masculine, but any animal would have scoffed with all the dirt he had accumulated. Now, he felt a little better, he felt more humanized. Jovan stuck his large callused hand under the water to watch it refract into two different dimensions. He then cleaned out from under his nails.

He was surely worried about having to wait naked in the forest to dry off. He used his shirt from the day before to get all the water and put his pants and his shoes back on. Judging by the sky and position of the sun, Jovan guessed it was still early, around nine AM. It would be another sweltering day, he figured. He dreaded the thoughts of just another thing making him breathless.

The walk back to his house seemed so long. He recognized that, somehow, in his drunken state, he ended up in the meadow where Samuel had had his last moments. The thoughts weighed so heavily on his conscious that he had just been led there, he figured.

Knights were never supposed to dwell on things. Knights were supposed to do whatever it would take for them to win, and coming out fighting still afterward. All of these years, he had thought, had begun to catch up with him.

When Jovan was nineteen, he had been knighted. It was a day for the whole noble community. He was kneeling down in front of the king, not knowing that when he rose, the whole kingdom that was around him would weigh heavily on his shoulders. After he rose that day, he had never been the same since. He became a man in a matter of days. His heart became tough and his ego soared like never before, but he got thrown quickly into reality. He remembered the first time he heard a horse cry out in agony- it was the same day he had come face to face with a dark reality, that he would have to do whatever it takes to survive.

And that was when the warrior inside him had been born. All his life he had mentally prepared himself for this moment, but it came with so much more than he ever thought. He became determined and strong- willed and he told himself that he would do whatever it takes to make it in a world of war.

Now, six years later, he was at the top of his game. He had come a long way since those first steps on the battlefield all those years ago. Now, he would flinch at nothing and dwell on everything.

Going back to his humble house would comfort him but it would not feel right. His life was for fighting, he knew, and not for being in love. He had no business falling for someone that would not catch him.

When he fell for her, he fell through time, he fell through clouds, he fell through layers of hard exterior. He had given it all up and given it a chance.

But he would go home now and try to forget it all and try to act as if nothing had happened.

He came home alone but at peace. His house was dark and quiet. What he needed now was to relax and take refuge in this quiet place. Out of all the places he had been recently, this had been the most peaceful. Even the meadow did not seem right anymore. There was a morbid, taunting presence that lurked there and put a dreadful feeling inside him.

As he walked in the door he spotted his crude bed over in the corner of the room, and the only thing he did before going straight to it was to close the door behind him. He walked over and nearly collapsed upon it. Right now, sleep would heal him and time would heal him. He knew he would just have to give them both a chance.

Jovan, unbelievably, had been able to find sleep. When he awakened, he felt more at ease and much calmer. He felt that today could be the first day of the rest of his life, and that he possibly could leave the past few weeks in the past, and they would be nothing but a distant memory.

Jovan rose that morning well rested and relaxed. It seemed that he could have another chance at things he thought he had screwed up beyond repair the day before.

A loud knock came to his door as he lay awake in his bed. He hesitated, not wanting to know who was there, not wanting to acknowledge the other people in the world right now. After a second of debating, Jovan lazily threw the covers off of himself and stretched out his whole body as he sat up on the side of the bed. He was bred so beautifully.

His broad muscles felt such relief as they were freely moved. He had such strength in his flawless chiseled form, such perfection in his flawless physique.

Two more knocks persisted at the door. Jovan sighed and rose. He put his green pants on as he walked to the door. He was hoping it was someone here to visit him, someone to check up on him and see how he had been doing. Maybe he could talk and visit with a long lost friend for awhile.

Or maybe it was bad news. The urgent sound of the knocking made him think that maybe it was something he would not want to hear. But Jovan was important and powerful- and he was needed all throughout the town. If something had happened, he would have to go deal with it.

So Jovan, mentally arming himself, opened the large wooden door. Immediately, hot summer wind blew into his house. Jovan was greeted by a young face, covered in black hair, with an icy blue stare looking back at him.

"Torin," he greeted, "Nice to see you." Torin looked desperately at him. "Thank you Sire," he responded, "I have a message for you." Here it comes, Jovan thought-some type of news he did not want to hear.

But what Jovan did not expect is that it was not that type of news at all- instead, it was shocking, it was insane, it was what he never thought he would have heard in a million years. It shook him to his core, left him standing at his door and spinning, his head in a place that his body was not.

"I have word from your father," Torin started, "He wants to see you."

Jovan's father- he was such a complicated man. Jovan had been pressured by him so much his entire life- Jovan's father had driven him insane. He, too, had been a knight- and he was determined that Jovan live up to what he never could accomplish- becoming a legend.

He had been a great knight, but he had been dehorsed in a jousting battle, disabling him after only a few years of fighting. He had severely broken his leg in numerous places and since then, had a limp whenever he would take a step. Growing bitter due to his condition, Jovan's father closed himself off from the world and became a drunkard. And now that Jovan had became what his father wanted, pressure and jealousy weighted on him hard.

"My father?" Jovan was baffled, he had not spoken to his father In years. "Did he say what it was about?" Torin shook his head. "No, sire, I believe it is a personal matter between the two of you. He said he would be expecting you this evening." "Thank you, Torin, I will meet with him." Jovan slammed the door though Torin still stood there at the threshold.

He ran his fingers through his hair again, a nervous habit he had adopted. His father? After all these years, this man had come out of nowhere. What was it that he needed to discuss? Maybe he would apologize, Jovan thought, after all the lost time, and he would be able to know his father again. It would be nice to have someone that cares for him, he thought.

But maybe it was a stretch to think these thoughts. He did not want to build himself up for great expectations and then be let down. When his father would drink, he would become violent and difficult. He was a terrible drunk, Jovan knew. When Jovan looked into the face of his father, he saw the same green eyes that he had but a tainted soul that he never wanted to share.

Jovan had felt sorry for his father but he had never known how to reach him. Now, he stood alone in his house, frozen with disbelief. His father had reached out to him. He had broken the silence after all these years.

Now Jovan had to make the next move. He would go, he thought, and listen to his father's words, and maybe he would understand. Jovan had always been his father's weakness.

The day Jovan had been born, it was the first day of Spring- a new beginning. The newborn had been brought to the king, wrapped in animal fur, but naked. The king had taken him up in his arms and looked Jovan dead in the eye, and saw through him. And right away, the king took off his crown and placed it atop Jovan's head. Of course the crown tilted to the side, as Jovan was an infant, and the crown was much too big, but all the nobles from around had gathered to look at the fine specimen of a child.

"He will be royalty, and noble," The king had spoken, with his gruff voice, that would still melt the heart of anyone listening, and make anyone else stop in their tracks. "He will fight many battles and bring much honor to our town. He will put fear into the hearts of many men, and be known from towns over. And we will be proud to call him our own."

And it was then that Jovan had gotten his name, because Jovan knew that the word meant 'majestic.'

And Jovan had begun to cry, and his father had taken him back from the king's hold. Jovan's father had a sparkle in his eye, so much pride that it radiated from him. His son, he knew, would lead armies and have no fear- and he would show him the way.

But he had never upheld his promise, because shortly after Jovan's birth his father had gotten his injury. As his mother had died giving birth to him and his father was on his deathbed, Jovan was nearly an orphan.

And after he had recovered but was unable to keep fighting, He became a bitter and miserable man. With Jovan, his temper had been short. He would watch his former fellow soldiers parade through town from their top-story townhouse window, and take long sips of alcohol. He taught Jovan to hunt at an early age, and Jovan often caught and killed whatever food they would have. But his father would always glare at him from across the table, a glazed look in his eye, and Jovan would often pass time with his father with no words.

As he got older, Jovan took to the woods more often, and had adventures on his own. His father would sometimes scold him for being gone for hours on end. And when he was sixteen, he became a squire, and got the first taste of his most lethal poison- knighthood.

Jovan's father was proud of him. But he was always very critical and always pressuring him to do more. For everything that Jovan accomplished, his father expected him to outdo it. One day, he had gotten into a fight with his father, after losing a joust, and Jovan's rage blew up. Jovan had been a ticking time bomb- building up negative energy with every disapproving action made by his father.

After his father had reached out to hit him, Jovan lost control and returned the action, leaving his father with a black eye, and then backing away to wonder what he had just done. Jovan had left the house and not spoken to his father since.

And that had been so many years ago. To hit a grown man was bad enough- but this had been his own father. The feelings of rage he would get from his father had been more than he could stand.

After years of his childhood with a drunkard, each day, one by one, slowly built onto one another until he was a person he himself no longer recognized.

So Jovan had never looked back. But today, he would walk back into that house with the crude wooden floors, he would look out the window that his father would stand and stare out of all those years ago. He would face green eyes of one of his greatest heartbreaks- the one that had been caused by his own flesh and blood.

Maybe he would get to make peace today. Maybe, Jovan thought, this was a sign that things would soon change and he would have a chance to restore the broken parts. He wanted to move on from all the things that had hurt him- all the lies and the games, all the hurt and the worry, all the times he had feared that he had done wrong- he wanted to be a new man. And he wanted to show his father what he had become.

Yes, Jovan was damaged; but he was also brilliant. From the time he had became a knight, he was so much stronger, so much wiser, so much better. His kaleidoscope eyes had seen many things. He had been dressed in the finest clothes, standing in the castle ballroom- and he had also been on his knees, covered in enemy blood, looking to God to save him.

He wondered if his father would be proud.

Jovan's heart skipped a beat; a little bit of anxiety went throughout his being. He knew he was good enough, but he did not know if his father could see it.

Jovan looked at himself in his big mirror and saw nothing but monsters. He saw the portrait of a hardened soldier, just like a river rock, he had been worn down with time and shaped into something so completely different.

That newborn baby had been the most humanistic form of him for his entire life. But the king had seen him fit, and the army respected him as a good and valued leader. So that must mean something, he thought.

Jovan got those old feelings again, suddenly, the ones he used to get from his father. The feelings came to the surface and he could feel nothing else. Jovan was frustrated and angered, and saddened all at the same time. His rage maneuvered his hand into a strong fist and he swung at his own reflection from the mirror in front of him.

Glass shattered and a crowd of birds quickly flew from a tree outside his window. The sharp, distinct sound rang incessantly in his ears. He pulled back a bloody fist, with tiny flecks of glass sticking in the wound bed. Jovan grabbed his fist with the other hand and held it in attempt to numb the pain.

This was temporary- all he could feel was sharp pain and see the crimson massacre running down his arm. Jovan backed up against the wall and then slid down it, collapsing onto the floor.

As he leaned back against the wall, he removed his shirt to wrap around the injured fist. And his mirror was also destroyed.

No one knew why those birds had flown away the way they did, or why there was broken glass now covering his floor. Jovan kept those secrets to himself, as he tried hard to make the best out of this brand new reality.

His father came into his life as soon as she had walked out. She had been his only sanctuary, and now demons surrounded him. The only thing he had done wrong was be born to the wrong man, and maybe he would have gotten her in the first place, and maybe he would have gotten a supportive father.

He loved his father- but it was a complicated love. And what would be hard for Jovan to understand is that his father loved him, too- love was the reason he had become so bitter and so cruel- because he had wanted to be good enough but never felt like he was.

Love, he knew, would be the worst poison. It would intoxicate the worst drunkard, it would overdose the most dedicated addict. It would drive the most intelligent person insane. And it made someone like him, a person with immeasurable strength, so weak and confused.

Whether it was love for his father or the love he had for Gracie, both kinds of love took hold of him and led him by the hand and by the heart, to places that he never would have otherwise gone.

He did not want to present himself to his father or to his town this way. He did not want to be the bloody hung over son of an old fighter- he wanted to show them all that he was just what they thought he was- a knight In shining armor.

Jovan moped around for awhile. He sat on his cold hard floor for a bit, and paced throughout his small house. He had spent the majority of the day confined to his house. He was ready now, he thought- he could face his father now and he could accept the situation. His angered emotion had now turned to ember, as the fire that had been burning was now extinguished.

Jovan attempted to dress appropriately. He was not much for fashion as he was a rugged man, but he had some of the finest clothes around of his time. He attempted to comb through his tangle of unruly hair. Jovan ran his fingers along his chin, as he was beginning to develop a slight stubble from not shaving for a few days.

He went out the door and started on the path that would change his life forever. After this, he knew, there was no looking back.

Sparrows circled above him as he stepped out into the Summer air. It welcomed him but it also taunted him as he walked further and further into it, becoming more constricting the further he got. The heavy air and his dramatic heartbeats were an elixir of anxiety on his weakened spirit.

Jovan had faced armies of men in his lifetime. He had been inches from faceless men, identity hidden by metal, the shadow of rage surrounding him, and he had never flinched. But the thought of facing his father, the man who had conflicted him all these years, gave him chills.

Jovan felt every foot step as he stepped slowly forward on the stone street. His heart would continue to lead him here as he knew that closure was what he needed. But, he wondered, what could he possibly need to speak with Jovan about? He knew it was something- but it could be anything.

As Jovan saw his father's house, he stopped for a minute to look up at it. The aura around the house was ghost-like. He knew such a big part of him was at this house, but it was a part he had left behind so long ago, and now it was here to haunt him. A faint glow came from that same upstairs window where his father used to sit.

The house was made of stone. It was small, but built up into two stories. He would have to walk through the town to get there- but at the outskirts, there it would be, stoically and patiently waiting for him to come back someday. It was stone and grey with a wooden shingled roof. There were three windows, made of thick glass, and today a candle in that window was the only light he saw anywhere around him.

Inside was a wood stove and two beds, one of which used to be Jovan's. The floors were wooden and crude. It was small but spacious. Jovan had been happy to grow up here- it was just the relationship he had had with his father that had pushed him away.

Jovan approached the door and brought up his fist to knock. And almost immediately, the door was opened.

Jovan stood in complete silence as he stared wide- eyed at the man who had given him everything he ever had- even his own life. Jovan's father had his same emerald eyes, a grey beard and Jovan's tall stature. His aging face began to soften as a slight smile appeared across his face. Crow's feet cornered his eyes and creased more as the smile became more genuine.

Then, suddenly, his father pulled him in and embraced him. Shocked, Jovan slowly wrapped his arms around his father. To think now that his father was so close to him was a surreal thought. Jovan's father maintained his tight grip on his son. His head was on Jovan's strong shoulders, his arms holding tight around Jovan's tortured body. His father started to softly sob. Tears soaked into Jovan's shirt. His heart fluttered.

"My son," he spoke. These were the first words that Jovan had heard his father speak since he left all those years ago. "My only flesh and blood! Let me look at you." He pushed Jovan back and looked him up and down. Jovan was the spitting image of this man.

"you are all I imagined you to be," he stated, "and all of a man now. You were so scrawny before." Jovan remained silent, though there was so much he wanted to say. It was difficult. They were supposed to put aside the past and talk as adults now. That was the difference between the way he was now and the way he was before- he was now a man, and he had to own up to what he had done, and he had to help heal the wounds that were his past.

"It's nice to see you too," Jovan replied, and he had suddenly realized something- he forgave him. He knew how emotions would change and shape a person, and his father was no exception. He forgave the anger and heartache. Suddenly, he felt he was home again.

"It has been too long," Jovan added. His father's smile remained as he opened the door for his son and motioned for him to come inside. Jovan took a few steps in and looked around at the interior. It was like stepping inside of a memory from long ago.

He stepped through it in a haze as he slowly put pieces together from all his times here. This was the period of innocence in his life- the time in his life before knighthood, before he had killed a man, before he romanced women all through the town.

He had just been himself, and he had been happy.

But his father had never let up on the pressure and eventually pushed Jovan away. From what he could see now, there was remorse in his father's eyes.

"Jovan, I just wanted to tell you that I am sorry for the way things were left. And I am so sorry for always being so hard on you. You are all that I have, and I never wanted to let you go, but once I saw that you would go I tried to hold you back. And now that I see what you have become, I could not be more proud."

Jovan blushed at this. "Father, I am no better than you once were," he replied. But his father cut in. "Son, I hear them chant your name in the streets. I see the castle from here and I see the lights and parties they have when wars have been won. I see the armies ride through and I see you at the front." Another tear came to his father's eye. "The soldiers I once fought with are no longer soldiers, but their sons now ride through during those parades. And I am so proud that you are one of them."

The volume of this weighed heavily on Jovan. He had had no idea how his father had admired him from afar. "Father, I always wanted your approval, I always wanted you to be proud of me. I had just always hoped that we could have seen eye-to- eye more often. That is one of my biggest regrets."

They sat now at the humble dining table near the window. He would be honest, he thought; he would finally say the things he had always wanted to say. There was nothing to hold back.

"Jovan I was not always the best to you. You deserved much better than me. God gave me you, though, and I was scared, I was afraid I would fail you as a father. And I believe I did. I am very sorry for that." "No," Jovan stopped him, "You did what you thought you had to do. Nobody knows the right thing for the moment. And it was hard to go on without my mother."

Jovan did not want to bring up his mother. It was a sore subject for both men. But it was true that his mother's death had been the root of most of his childhood angst and part of the reason his father had been so bitter. Jovan had no memory of his mother, since she had died when he was born. But he knew she had been a loving woman and she had been thrilled to become a mother. She had had long dark hair, Jovan had been told, and warm dark eyes.

But now that she was gone, Jovan was all his father had left. "Yes it was, and after I got hurt I was never the same. I felt foolish for bringing you into such a messed up world. But you were mine and I knew I needed to do the best I could for you, and I still wanted you to become a knight, even though I was no longer myself."

Though Jovan had a love-hate relationship with knighthood, he could not imagine what he would do if it were suddenly taken away from him. Knighthood was his whole identity. He was born and built to fight; he was in his comfort zone on the back of his horse, wearing his sparrows and adrenaline rushing through his bloodstream. If he had all that taken away from him, he would be nothing but a drunken recluse with battle wounds in his backwoods home.

"I know it must have really been terrible to have it all taken away from you at once, and feeling like you have lost control of everything. I know having me there must have only made things harder. And it takes me being a knight myself to realize that," Jovan said, letting it all out. "And being a fighter has taken a lot of things away from me.

It has taken my freedom, my sanity, and my innocence. But I never wanted it to take you. And for a long time, I thought that it had. And I never had the courage to come see you again after all the things that had happened between us. But I always loved you. You are my father and nothing that happens will ever change that."

When Jovan would fight, he would keep in his mind the things that he was fighting for. He would always think about surviving, for one. Each day he woke up again with sun rays on his face and the wind blowing through his hair, when he laughed and loved and talked with his friends, he was grateful. But he was also grateful for those he loved. He would think of his father, then quickly shake the thought from his head; Because one day he hoped to see him again, but he was not sure how. And today here he was with him and he had everything to say with no reason to hold back.

Jovan's father put his head down and cupped his face in his hands. Closure was a beautiful thing. Now after they would mend their jagged edges, they could never have these feelings again.

But Jovan was not one to show emotion and neither was his father. It was a flaw in his otherwise perfect design.

"Thank you, son," the old man finally responded. "Just know that I never forgot you. You saved me, Jovan." He said. "You gave me hope and a reason to live. After my injury when I felt so close to death, I would feel myself slipping away and think about how you needed me, and pray to God that I could stay here, just a little bit longer, to be with you. And he gave me all these years. And you showed me that there is something bigger to this life, something better, something fulfilling. I never felt whole until I held you in my arms. And for you to be such a great warrior, gives me so much pride and so much happiness. I know your future is bright, son. I just hope that you have not given up on me and that you can look past the way I used to be. I am humbled now, and I see that I may not have many years left, and I want to spend the last years I have as someone that you value in your life."

Jovan was glad that his father had been the one to gather the courage to bandage these old wounds and give some peace to his aching soul. For a man that never showed his emotions, he was putting everything on the line to earn Jovan's forgiveness. But Jovan wondered, why, after all these years, was he suddenly saying these things? And if he had so much pride, why was he never present at parades, or jousts, or castle parties in which he was always invited to but never came? Why had he never made an effort to acknowledge him rather than admire his success from afar?

Though Jovan hoped so, he wondered if his father's words were said in earnest. Their complicated history had led them here, at this wooden table in a townhouse, speaking all their feelings from years ago. But Jovan still had his guard up. He had refused to be completely vulnerable around this man. Though he knew him very well, Jovan had the feeling there were things he did not know about him, and for some reason, Jovan could not help but feel suspicious. The good feeling he had had inside him had now gone away- and he began to feel like maybe he had not been so quick to allow his father to see this side of him.

Jovan met his father's gaze. Today was a lifetime of questions answered- and Jovan wanted all of the answers.

"Father," he said calmly, "Just tell me- why did you call me here?"

Jovan's father swallowed hard. He grabbed the table for support, as if he might fall out of his chair. "The things I said before were all things I wanted to say. And I am glad that you know now. But there is another reason for why I had you come here."

Jovan felt a large, stabbing pit in his stomach. He felt betrayed. This was what he had feared- not that his father wanted his forgiveness and their relationship to be repaired, but instead to expose another shred of reality to him he did not want to realize.

He was livid. He wanted badly to walk out the door again and walk out of his father's life. But he waited to see what would come next.

What Jovan did not know, though, is that these next few words would change his life forever. It would send him into a dazed spiral and make him sick to his stomach, and tie him to so many things he wanted to escape from.

"Jovan, I-" He stopped for a second, then upon seeing Jovan's anxious gaze, continued. "I think you deserve to know what I have been wanting to tell you. You are a man now, and you are a great one. And in order for us to have a new start, I need to tell you all the things that have weighed on me all these years."

Jovan felt like it was taking forever for his father to say it. Seconds were like hours at this point in time.

"Samuel was your brother."

Just then, all of the color flushed from Jovan's body. Time stopped, and everything around him was silent.

Had he heard right? Had the man that had pinned him with a sword been his own flesh and blood? Had the darkened soul he knew as Samuel been more than just his brother in arms?

If it was true, it made sense- they had the same skill, the same statue- like build, the same desire to uphold their honor.

Had Samuel known? Had that been the reason he had treated Jovan so badly their whole time fighting together?

It took Jovan a minute to find his words. But at this point, he did not know if he ever wanted to utter any other word to his father for the rest of his life.

Jovan's father had pleading eyes. He begged for a reaction from his son, he begged for some type of understanding. But Jovan had closed his mind, he had shut his father out. He knew all he needed to know.

"Son, I have to tell you what happened," his father finally said, after Jovan did not speak. "I used to be in love with Samuel's mother. We met at a parade in town and after I saw her, I could not get her out of my head. But I knew that I could never be with her. She was betrothed to another man. But we began to have an affair, and found that she was pregnant. There was no chance that I could stay. There was no chance that I could let that ruin my reputation, and possibly risk my whole career. So I left. Samuel's mother married her betrothed before everyone knew she was pregnant, and the man believed that Samuel was his son; but he was killed in battle shortly after Samuel was born and he and his mother were left with nothing.

That is when she began to work for the king and Samuel grew up in the castle, where he eventually got introduced to knighthood. Samuel never knew that his mother's husband was not his real father. By this time, I was married to your mother, and not even she knew; and you were born right afterward."

Jovan could not believe his ears. What his father had basically confessed to was shocking. It had been his father's darkest secret, one that he would have taken to his grave. Only three people had ever known the truth- his father, Samuel's mother, and God above. The two of them had loved one another so that they never spoke of their deadly secret.

And the most insane thing of all- except for the pregnancy, Jovan's affair had been just the same as the one his father had had. Jovan could not fathom how this could have happened. Samuel's life had begun and ended with a secret love affair. Had his life been built around lies?

Jovan was shaking, he felt as if he would vomit. He felt like he could fuel a thousand fires with the anger he now possessed.

"It was nice to see you, father, but I see that you have not changed much," Jovan managed. He stood and pushed his chair in. His father begged to him as he began to walk out, asking him not to leave, to stay and talk and maybe he would understand. But Jovan was not able to face him right now. The only thing that Jovan could understand was why his father had been such a drunk.

Nothing Jovan had said to his father had been false. He had loved him and he had forgiven him. But he could not help but wonder if his father meant anything he had said to him, because he had so easily lied to him his entire life.

If Jovan had known, he maybe could have had a friendship with Samuel. He maybe could have shared something with him that he would share with no one else. But now, Samuel lay in a hollow grave In the mountains. He had been buried with honor, surrounded by his fellow soldiers, but he had been laid to rest never to breathe another breath or fight another fight.

Jovan was not sure if he would be able to walk home. He fought the urge to seek alcohol; because he knew it would not solve his problems- nothing would ever solve this. Jovan felt anger toward his father for the decisions he had made to alter the lives of so many other people.

But how could he be mad, he thought- he had done the exact same thing. Except his affair had been different- he had taken the lover of his one and only brother, and tainted his own honor, and brought shame to his inner self. No one would ever know, he thought- he could continue to live his life. But Samuel did not have that luxury. Samuel had been damaged in so many ways, and had never even known it.

Jovan himself had honor to uphold, and would have been badly punished if anyone had found out about he and Gracie. So he was able to understand how his father may have panicked when he was made aware of the pregnancy. But Jovan himself knew that a man had to be accountable for his actions, and he would have never been able to abandon his child in such a way.

Jovan knew the men in his bloodline must be flawed- he shared more problems with his father than he had ever known. But he knew that in his situation, he would be much better off keeping his secret to himself.

Though the feeling he had gotten from their talk had angered, shocked, and shaken him, he was glad that he now knew- he now knew the truth that had always evaded him. But he still did not understand why Samuel possessed such hatred, why such animosity was held toward Jovan.

Jovan guessed it was maybe due to their equal fighting skill and equal social status; to match skill such as theirs was very rare. Samuel was always trying to outdo Jovan, and rise to the top. But their skill and strength, courage and intelligence had been so much the same because they had both inherited it from the same person.

Missing pieces were beginning to come together, but there would always be gaps in between; because even though Jovan had finally found out about his past, he would still never completely understand. No one else would ever understand his misery or why he would lay awake at night. Because even though he now knew the truth, his brother never would. And he had spent his whole career fighting beside a man that shared more with him than he could have dreamed of.

The walk back to Jovan's house was more lonely than it had been before. There were no lights around now, the sky was beginning to turn dark and the calling of frogs and insects had replaced that of the songbirds. Though they were loud, the world seemed silent. It seemed like such a perilous place to be. The world was so corrupted by people and their wicked ways, and he imagined there were so many secrets this world would never know- they would only be known by those that had lived them and tried to forget. He was now one of those people. He now had two dangerous secrets to keep. Seeing his father had not been at all what he had expected. But he never knew what to expect when he saw the man that was such a big part of him and the way that he was.

If anything, he had made amends with him and he knew that after he recovered from this shock, he would finally be able to make peace with one of the most complicated people his life had given him. It made him so grateful that he had been the lucky one-but also a little guilty. He could have easily been in Samuel's place. But God had given him this life. He was still living and breathing and he still had a chance to make peace with his own soul and with Samuel's spirit. That was the only thing he could do to make things right.

The last image he had of Samuel flashed through his mind. He saw him high up on his hazel stallion, dressed in full battle attire, and leading the charge up to the top of the castle. He saw the other knights in a colorful flash of color around him as they too galloped into the castle. They showed the enemy they had no fear, and they were not backing down. They had been fearless and valiant, and led by Samuel.

Jovan felt a dagger of emotion radiate throughout him. On Samuel's last day, he had fought as hard as he could, he had put everything he had into that battle. It had been his destiny to lead them, because he had led them to victory- and he never knew that his numbered hours were slowly being counted down.

Jovan had always known the feelings that were had after Samuel's death been intensely saddening and morbid. Now he knew the reason why.

The fact that Jovan had had an affair just like his father was something that he could not get past. Both men had been lured in by beautiful forbidden loves, and put them above everything else in their lives. Both men had let these women take them out of their dreaded realities, but they both were soon awakened with a bigger problem than before. Guilt and remorse could destroy them both.

Jovan had a lot to process tonight. But even now, some of his questions remained unanswered. There was still one person he needed to confront, a girl he never cared to see again- it was River.

Jovan would have to open many doors in order to close old ones. He wanted the secrets and evil in his past to wither and die. These small things had so much control over him, he knew; and he wondered if it would ever end.

In order for him to end it all, he would have to face everything head on, and handle it with courage, just like he did in his fights. If only he could fight physically, instead of mentally- he would have no problem handling it that way.

He still had to figure out why River had chose to get involved in his business, and risk both their lives by meddling. The thoughts of her siren face led chills throughout his body. He lost his grip on reality when she was nearby. She was nothing but bad news. Somehow he would have to confront her and maintain his composure while doing it. He could not let her use her searing stare to cut through him; he could not let her touch melt through his mortal skin and complicate his thoughts. She was a goddess that could put even the most sane man under a wicked spell. He knew it would not be easy.

Her stare could make an army of men shake with hypnotic wonder. She was mesmerizing and beautiful and so dark. Her silver tongue cut through him when she spoke, demonic eyes voiding his mind of all other thoughts. Her thirst was manic. Her hunger was eternal. Being her must be hell, he thought, because she was forever chasing something she could not have.

Jovan hoped no one would ever be able to venture into the inner workings of his mind. He never wanted anyone to know how disturbed he was, how he wondered if he was actually losing his mind. But the desire to overcome and understand all the complicated things would keep him going and push him further than he would ever go.

Chapter 7

Now that he had discovered so many missing pieces of his past, he knew he had to figure out the rest. Images of his entire life flashed through his mind- images of the castle, a timeless never-changing image posed against a periwinkle sky. He saw images of his army- mortal souls just like him, no stronger or more courageous than he, but just as much so. They would be fully armed and riding strong, though, horses in position perfectly. He saw Gracie's smile. It killed him on the inside to know that the only way he would ever see it again would be in his memory. These were the things he held most dear in his life, and the reasons he wanted to make things right- so he knew he had to make the next move.

Jovan knew where he could find River. She would be at her house near the ocean, but if he waited, she would come out to walk along the beach and gather seashells. Each day, he knew, she would be there. However, tomorrow, she would find him waiting for her.

Jovan woke ready to confront her. Though the knowledge of his past had shaken him, it had given him an odd type of strength and he wanted to put it all to rest. River would no longer have a grip on him and he would get freedom he had not had from her since they had met. He had seen the lustful look in her eye more than enough to know what her intentions were. He would finally put an end to the dirty feelings she gave him and confront her about the meddling she had done.

He sat on the edge of his bed gripping his injured hand from the previous day's rage attack. Staring out into the distance, he mentally prepared himself. He would not try to change things; he would just try to understand.

River would never hurt him. She cared for him and wanted him, and admired him greatly. Her greatest fault was how she had begged for him, how she longed to be in his muscled hold, how she would blindly do anything for him because she loved him so. River was the type of girl that would forever be there for him.

Forever to her was just that- an eternal flame that would burn hot for him for as long as she would live. What she did not know, however, is that flame would burn both of them in the end.

It was a candle burning at both ends, and when it reached the middle, it would set flame to everything around it, and destroy whatever it touched.

Jovan stepped out and for the first time the entire summer, a chill graced his body. He could see it in his mind now, her ember eyes warmer than the afternoon sun, mesmerizing him. As he began walking her whispering words seemed to echo with the wind in the trees. He could hear her words in his mind.

"Dance with me, Jovan."

And that was what had started it all.

Her petite hands had held to him with all the strength they possessed. Her curves were pressed tight against him. The undying lust flickered in her eyes as he had danced away the night with her. She had known he did not desire her as she desired him. But her heart had ached for him and her hope to be with him had still endured.

As Jovan walked toward the ocean, he looked behind him to see the town he had loved and protected. The castle's proud golden and red flag wavered gallantly above all else around him. For those colors he had shed his blood, he had sacrificed his youth, and he had done It all with so much love. With just as much nobility as he had done these things, he walked onward to face one of his biggest vices.

He walked the path he had come with Gracie their first night together. As he began to get closer, he could hear the angry waves crash against the shore. Today was a crazy day for the tides. He walked down to the clearing where he could just see the ocean. As he looked over and down onto the shore, there he saw her. From a distance, she looked just like any other girl. Her crimson hair blew all around her in the ocean wind. She was bending over as she grabbed a shell and placed it in her basket. She had no idea he was watching her; but seeing her in this state seemed to make her more human. To watch her was enticing. It was as if she were a whole other person. But, he knew what lay beneath that innocent exterior. And today he would put an end to it all.

Jovan walked out on the beach and stood there, waiting for her to look up. And when she looked up, her hair blew across her face and covered her eyes for a second. When she moved it out of her face, he could see the spark immediately. And his heart skipped a beat. He was speechless. He had had everything in his mind that he wanted to say to her; but now that they were face-to-face, it had all evaded him. She was shocked to see him. "Jovan," she breathed, shocked enough to drop the basket of shells and send them tumbling back on the sand. Her toes were covered in the sand and her nose blistered from the wind.

"What are you doing here?" Jovan had his hands resting in his pockets as he faced her. "I came to talk to you. There are a lot of things we need to clear up. I need you to open up to me about what has been going on." "What do you mean?" she asked, defensively. "I need you to tell me why you would report to the other soldiers, and to Torin, that I was too sick to fight. Before the battle, you spread the word that I should not be alerted of the siege that Januvia was attempting on our castle. And I want you to know that that was a dangerous move."

Her jaw had dropped and her face turned pale. "River, if they had fought that battle without me, I would lose my credibility as a knight. And you know that everything I do must uphold my honor. Why would you put me in a place like that?"

She approached him and ran her hand seductively down his chest. His hard exterior began to melt. "Tell me, Jovan," she started, "is that really why you came here?"

Jovan pushed her away and shook his head. "River. You interfered with a battle going on here. Do you have any idea how serious that is?" River rolled her eyes. "You know I would never hurt you," she replied. "You know that, don't you Jovan?" Jovan was appalled at just how calm she remained even after knowing what she had done. "River, the games are over. I can never love you. I wish my heart was not so set in it's ways, but I have to chase after what I want and you are not the one I love. You were always a great friend to me. And you will always have me to fight for you and look out for you. But we could never be together."

"Yes," she finally managed, "yes, I did try to keep you away from the battle that day. But not because I thought you couldn't fight. I was just- trying to protect you." Jovan dared her with a questioning glance. "What do you mean, River? Protect me from what?" She looked down to the sandy footprints she had created and began to fidget within one with her big toe. "River," he stated, her name was like lava on his lips, "answer me."

"Nothing," she replied, "I didn't mean to say that. I didn't need to protect you from anything." Jovan put his hand on her shoulder. "River, look me in the eye and tell me. What is going on?" "I didn't want you to see!" She exclaimed suddenly. "See what?" Jovan demanded, yelling back at her.

"I didn't want you to see him die."

Jovan's blood ran cold and he began to shake all over. A dreaded, eerie feeling rushed over him. The sky seemed to get a little darker and the sea a little fiercer. Though River usually burned through him, today she was cold as ice.

"Samuel," she said, "I didn't want you to see him die." Jovan's look was puzzled and full of shock. River stumbled over her words. "I need you to hear me out," she began. "I know you never loved me. But you loved her instead." Jovan shuttered at how she could not say Gracie's name, "but no matter what, I loved you from the start. I loved you so much, Jovan, always. And you never made it easy. You always made me fight for you and long for you. But when I saw I could never have you, I felt I would rather die than live without you. So I did the only thing I could do- I decided to let you be happy. I love you so much, Jovan, that all I really want is you to be happy. So I did it."

Jovan was afraid of what would come next. But he asked the question anyway. "What did you do, River?" and just like that, her smoldering eyes flooded with crystalline tears.

"I killed Samuel. I knew that if he was dead, you could be with her. And that was what you had truly wanted." Jovan felt his heart drop immensely and his whole body go numb. The feeling he had was surreal- surely this could not be actually happening. Would she really do something like this? Would she really let her love for him get the best of her so that she would actually cause another soldier's death? Jovan held his face in his hands. He, too, began to cry. Nothing had made him cry until now- he had went his whole career as a knight and never cried once. But now, tears fell from his eyes, into the sand, only to be washed away by the furious ocean.

"Because I loved you Jovan," she tried again. "If she was what you wanted, I wanted you to be able to have her. I knew she would marry Samuel soon and the two of you would never be together." It had been true, Jovan knew, that the wedding would have already happened by now and Gracie would be Samuel's wife, and he would never get to be with her. But that was never worth another man's life. Though Gracie's presence was beyond powerful and meant everything to him, he still would have never wanted Samuel to die because of it.

There was no way to fix this, Jovan knew. Nothing would ever bring Samuel back and nothing would erase the past. These were the things he would never be able to accept. Samuel had never deserved what had happened to him because all he had done wrong was love the wrong person- just as Jovan had done. The two men, however, received very different outcomes.

Jovan choked back his tears as he faced River again. Her face was difficult for him to look at. "River, I'm not happy. Samuel being dead does not make me happy. You have killed one of Hawthorne's greatest soldiers. You have brought sadness all throughout this land. Gracie has gone home back to her town now that he is gone, and I will still never be with her. What you have done is unspeakable.

Nothing will change it, and nothing will make it right. I never thought you would do such a thing."

The tears she cried for him were in vein. She was selfish and she knew he could never love her the way she loved him. Her heart ached with greed and desire, because he was so beautiful in her eyes. And now, as her vision was blurred with tears, she looked at her object of affection as his jade eyes gazed toward the ever changing waters.

"Why can't I make you love me," she cried hysterically; and Jovan knew that her heart had ached for him and he had been a king in her mind. In River's mind, Jovan was above all others. He was exceedingly beautiful but hopelessly unattainable. He was the hero in his town, she thought, and she had hoped that he could save her too.

But Jovan could not even save himself.

"The dance in the ballroom," he started, "It was all a mistake." The whole night had been a mistake- that had been the first night he had laid eyes on his fair skinned beauty and pursued her the whole night, while he had fueled the fire of the one that truly loved him only to abandon her.

Jovan's sullen half-brother had later returned to retrieve his betrothed from the hands of a man that had no intention of ever letting her go.

"You were all a part of this," he had slipped out. "You had no business being involved, but you chose to be. You could not stand that I didn't want you. And you didn't accept it, you just pushed yourself into my life when you were not welcome."

River did not understand the noble world, though she was part of it. She did not understand the unspoken codes of knighthood, the social ethics. She did not understand the love Jovan had possessed. She had loved Jovan with so much passion that it had killed her on the inside, and she had to do something about it. And though she would not sleep beside him at night, she would still sleep soundly knowing that she had listened to her heart.

But Jovan's sadness had turned into rage, and he found himself yelling when he spoke. "I never want to see you again. To get yourself involved in something that you were never even a part of is insane.

And you have no idea how serious these things are. Knighthood is not something to toy with," he continued, "there is no need for meddling girls when a battle is going on in our town."

Knighthood was about honor and integrity, honesty and respect. With someone like River interfering, it was not possible to stick to these values; because her intention was to intervene, just to gain what she had wanted.

And Jovan did not understand her love. He had never had someone love him so much that she would kill for him. Her love was unchanging, steady, and everlasting. He ran from her love because she had been so sure about it. But now as he looked into her pain stricken gaze with the ocean water spraying up on him, he could see that he had torn her heart into pieces. And he knew her love had been real.

"All I ever wanted was you," she said, "and all I got was pushed away. And it put me at my breaking point. I don't understand why you liked her so much. But I can't help that. If you would never love me, I wanted you to at least be happy. But now I see that neither of those things will ever happen."

Jovan was angry with her, and he was hurt. He was saddened and he was betrayed. The girl whom he had seen as somewhat of a younger sister had stabbed him in the back more crudely than any soldier with malicious intent ever could. Jovan knew all he needed to know. He knew River's character and he knew her blackened heart. No matter which way he looked at it, there was extreme sadness in every part of the situation. He knew he had been cold toward her in the beginning, but he had never had any intention of drawing her in, just to let her down even more. And with the feeling finally returning to his body, he said one last thing to her before he left: "Goodbye, River." And at that, he turned to stalk away back into the town.

She ran after him, calling and begging for him to come back; but Jovan was moving onward. He had nothing left to say to her. She had created a huge stain on his otherwise clean lifestyle. She was part of the secrets, he thought. She had added another forbidden secret to the Hawthorne nobility. People would live and die and never know the real truth. But every so often, when she lay in bed at night and was alone with her thoughts, she would think about what she had done, and it would haunt her for the rest of her days. And that was good enough for Jovan.

So many men had died at the hand of another in this day and age. Few had lived through those battles, only to be killed by a scorned enemy or a jealous rival. Samuel had lived his life around the lies of the people who were supposed to love him. He had been the product of a forbidden affair from the start. His biological father had abandoned him to go on to raise his other son, which had been his mortal enemy; who was the same man to begin another affair- that of which would end his life. Samuel's life had been built around lies and affairs had started and ended his life here. Knighthood had been his true love, what he really lived for, and what he had put all of himself into no matter what. And now, Jovan and his fellow soldiers would fight even harder from now on; because they would think about their dead comrades and know that they would be proud. They would fight hard for them, to honor their spirits, because in the life of a knight, that was the most important thing.

Chapter 8

Jovan had returned home and sat on his bed, and stared out of his window. How, he wondered, could anyone have the capacity to kill for a reason such as the one River had? Why had he been so unforgettable to her, and why had she fallen for him the way she had? The girl Jovan had loved the most had been the one to easily walk away; while the one he had rejected had killed for him. Jovan's life had taken an interesting turn of events. He had an honest soul, but the things life confronted him with had taken away some of his honesty. No words would ever let Samuel know that he was truly sorry. Nothing would ever change the fact that they had not been friends. If he could see Samuel now, he would not tell him all the forbidden things that surrounded his life; instead, he would sit quietly beside him and tell him how he admired his skill and that he was so sorry that his life had been so hard on him. And maybe they could have reached an understanding.

Jovan looked down at his injured hand, still aching from the day before. His hands told the story of his life. Every crease and fold of them had bruises, calluses, splinters and dirt. Dirt was under his nails, and he looked at it, as he regretted knowing all he had been through. Sea wind had made his lips dry, summer sun had made his skin dark; and so much alcohol had made his stomach weak.

Jovan thought back to Gracie, and how everything about her was painfully beautiful. He had cradled her chin in his large hand, and she had seemed so petite to him, and so delicate; yet she could tear him down in a second, and weaken him greatly. Maybe, he thought, this was what it was all about- giving so much of yourself to someone, that if they ever left you, a huge part of yourself would never be whole again. Jovan thought this was so beautiful. Loving her had been taboo, but it had been what his heart had longed for, and so he gave in.

He wondered if this was how his father had felt when he had met Samuel's mother. He wondered if it pained him everyday not being able to be with her, to see his own son be claimed by another man, and to know that the world would never know the love they shared.

Echoes of his youth came into his mind. He could hear his father's voice, just like it was yesterday. "Show them, young blood. Do this for Hawthorne."

"See, Jovan? These are the reins. Hold tight to them and never let them go."

And the worst but perhaps most truthful of all:

"Breathe, Jovan, and you won't feel the pain."

His father had coached him to be the man he was today, though they were nothing alike. And he would always see his other son riding alongside Jovan, wearing the same colors, and always holding his breath.

He heard Gracie's voice- "My soldier, my one and only. Love me like bees hunger for honey, thirst for me like ravens at the spring. But hold me like I am your eternity."

Then Samuel's baritone rushed through his memory. "Get up, and fight me, like a true man would," he heard, and he remembered Samuel's sword in his face and the way he had lain on the forest floor, as sparrows had soared above him.

Fighting, Pushing, Praying, Wanting, Loving, Needing, Knowing- all of it sent racing thoughts in his mind, and he knew there was no escape. It was a reality he had created for himself, his own fantasy; a fantasy of a thousand colors, a thousand lifetimes, a thousand chances. The fault was inside of him- he had been a lover and a warrior bound together in one soul. The only thing that had separated him from the warrior he was had been his capacity to love.

There was so much to it. When he had survived a battle, dirty and tortured, but still alive, he had understood. It all came together to form the beautiful soul that he was- the strength in his eyes, the sound of his voice, the days of his life- everything he had and the ability to use it. The wind, the water, the trees. The difference in loving someone and lusting after them. He could come clean and tell the king what River had done, but he knew it would not bring any goodness to the kingdom.

The king was a very kind and elderly man. All of Jovan's life, he had been under the rule of the same king. But when it came to business of the courts, he was extremely serious and he would issue a very serious punishment. Jovan knew that telling on River would also result in telling on himself. And he had so much to lose if he were to do that. Likely, Jovan knew, he would lose his place as a knight, and those that loved and admired him so would look down on him greatly. He would likely end up in shackles at the town square and become taunted for his affairs.

River, however, would be imprisoned and possibly put to death for her murder. The killing of a knight of Samuel's status was a very serious matter and she would likely never be released from the medieval torture prison. People of Hawthorne would see her crime as a disservice to their army, because Samuel had been such a valued knight, and they would show her no mercy.

Some things, he knew, were meant to be handled by the knights that faced them. They had no business in the courts. He would not bother the king with his own problems. He could face the things that came to him on his own.

Now, Jovan wanted to do as he usually did on nights like these and drown himself in alcohol. And instead of stopping himself, he went back to his old habit. Jovan walked past the shards of glass still covering his floor and rifled through his pantry, pulling out a jug of ale. There was dust on the jug and it was certainly heavy- it had sat for years in its place, patiently waiting for his desperation to bring him to it. Jovan was clad only in his tan pants and black leather boots. He looked sloppy as he walked from his house, almost forgetting to shut the door behind him, and holding tightly to his jug, half-dressed with his hair blowing all around in the summer winds.

He walked out to see the woods in the distance before him. So many things had happened there. It had been his childhood retreat, it had been a consoling solace for him. It had also been where many battles had taken place, where many men had died and many secrets were held. The place that brought so much beauty to Hawthorne had also brought much sadness.

The medieval forest seemed so dark and forbidden now. The thick trees seemed so daunting, so threatening as the black silhouettes of the trees were stamped into the sky around them. Jovan took his first drink and felt the burn. He wanted it to burn him from the inside, to intoxicate him to a point of no return. As he turned to walk through the town, he could see the faint glow of candles coming from a few houses. The castle was dark and still for the night. It stood tall as always, gallant and beckoning in the night. Jovan knew that tomorrow, servants would be up early, cleaning and decorating, preparing for another banquet.

It was just like the banquet where he had danced with River and seen Gracie for the first time. After that, his life would never be the same. And tomorrow, he knew he would be there at the long wooden table, with all his jovial men except Samuel's seat would be empty. River would shoot him searing looks from across the room; and he would have to act like everything was ok. But inside, he knew it was not ok. It took a certain amount of strength to face certain things, he knew.

To see his enemies in the same room with his friends, to accept honor and praise after he knew the dirty truth, to live a noble life with all the secrets that were kept within the noble society- it was never easy. Being a knight was being many things, but it was also being mindful of the things you knew and kept to yourself. Don't get too close to anyone, he knew, because something nasty might happen. It was a world of war and adversity, and kings and blood and brothers, and to get too personal and too involved with them was a risk in itself. You would find out things you did not want to know and you would have many secrets collected that you could never share.

Gold would make the palace shine; red would be streamed throughout the room, magnolias and their scent would be placed in every corner. The funny jester would make jokes and play his French horn. The king would sit high on his throne, wearing his furs and silver jewels, and praise the men for their sacrifice and their skill. Jovan was not sure if he would feel any joy. The past few days had given him a sickening feeling and he felt that he may vomit.

Now, he felt a buzz from the alcohol. It was all he needed to take the edge off. Why did he do this to himself, he wondered; why did he turn to a bottle when things got hard? It could never save him; it could only drown his sorrows, as the sea would drown drunken sailors. He was no different. He had never claimed to be any more than he was, however it seemed that he was not as strong as he had always thought.

Jovan walked past his father's house. He stood to stare for a minute. There was a candle glowing from that certain window. He knew his father probably sat there, as he had every night for the past twenty years, watching and waiting for something better. Jovan began to feel the stabbing pain of anger shoot through him. His father had been a foolish man. In his life he had only put knighthood first instead of being a father. He had sacrificed Jovan to be a soldier just as he had been and he had pressured him until he was broken. He had given up his firstborn in order to protect his own knightly image. He had lived his whole life as a lie but no one would ever know. Jovan's life had been lived by honor and by courage. He had upheld his image as cleanly as he could have. But the corrupt people that were in his life had damaged him, broken him, and he was not sure he could ever be the same again.

By now the alcohol had hit him hard. Jovan knew that there had to be more to life than this. When he had been led somewhere, he now knew it was meant to be. So he knocked on the door.

Jovan's father came to the door with bags under his eyes. He, too, had been drinking. Jovan held up the jug and smiled. "Want to share?" he had asked. His father smiled and welcomed him in. "My son," he had said, his voice shaky. "I never thought I would see you again." Jovan stared back at him through bloodshot eyes and said nothing. His father continued. "But this is not the way I hoped you would be if I ever did."

Jovan burped as the alcohol now began to affect his entire body. "Father, you are the reason I am the way that I am. And I cannot apologize for the way things are. But I do want you to know that I forgive you."

Jovan's father stood facing him in the kitchen, green eyes looking back at him. His facial expression was shocked. "Jovan, I never expected you to forgive me. The things I did-there were no excuse for. And if I had the chance, I would still do it again. Because of my mistake, another legend was born, just like you." Jovan sat his jug down on the nearby kitchen table. This was all he had needed to hear, he thought; Samuel had been born because he was meant to be here, he was meant to fight alongside Jovan and make a name for himself.

"There are things that I have done that I am ashamed of. I've made mistakes too and I know that there is nothing now that I can do to change it. And I am upset with you, but I know that there are things we can do to move on." Jovan knew the sad reality- his father was now all he had left. Aside from him, he had no other family or anyone else to love him. Though forgiving his father took a great deal of swallowing his pride, Jovan knew it was what he had to do to find peace within his soul.

Jovan's father got a glass and held it out for Jovan to pour some of his jug into. The stuff poured like gold into his father's glass, flowing smoothly out of its container. Jovan had been led here. Coming to see his father had not been his intention. But his drunken stupor and his aching body had led him to this house, and his heart had told him to go inside. This was something else that was meant to be, he thought.

Maybe, there was no reason for the things that had happened. Maybe, he thought, they were just all meant to be. There was no question for the things that God put into place.

He sat with his father in silence for awhile. They sat and drank. It was a silent understanding. They now had closure for the past. Jovan could see the future as brighter than his past had been. He could move on from their petty misunderstanding from his childhood. Jovan wondered if this was what being a man was like, putting the hard things aside and being able to accept them even though it may be hard.

Jovan stayed at his father's house for hours. He went out and began to set out to wherever else he may be led. The feeling he got from reconciling had made him feel light as feathers- it was the best feeling he had gotten in a really long time, it was the purest he had felt since he could remember.

He kept a hold to his jug as he set out on the town again. Why he did this, he would never know. Walking through the town, he thought, reminded him of why he did what he did. It gave the idea and the romance of knighthood a level of humanity, a realistic approach as to what knighthood was really about.

Jovan began the walk down to his woodland house. Maybe, he would get some sleep after all. Maybe, he would sleep soundly now that one thing in his life had finally been taken care of. River, however, was a person whom we thought he may not be able to forgive. She had been so cunning and so selfish. Her own desires had overshadowed what should have mattered the most to her. The well-being of her kingdom was jeopardized by her own personal gain. And here Jovan was, left with nothing-Gracie had still left him and now, he would never see her again.

When Jovan returned home, he sat on his bed for awhile and enjoyed being surrounded by silence. He knew that he could fix things if he needed to.

Jovan got up and took his finest silk shirt from the closet. It was maroon, and made of the smoothest rich silk. He knew he would have to prepare himself for this banquet, just as he prepared himself for every battle he had ever fought. Jovan would live another day to fight and to be a legend in this town. He would live another day to stand in the face of danger, to look death in the face, to fight for all those that could no longer fight beside him.

The last banquet had been what started it all. It was the first night he had seen her- his beautiful angel that had been sent to this earth to shoot him down with cupid's arrow. His scornful, envious, raging, fiery and lustful devil of an acquaintance, that could never have enough of him, so she broke him down into a fraction of the man he once was. There was his men- a jovial group; a bright, loving, and boisterous crowd. They upheld one another and they were so glorious. They were what made Hawthorne what it was- they were the core of it, the protectors, the fearless leaders that constantly sought infinite victory.

They gave hope to this oppressed town. They made the grey landscape bright with their red and golden flags; they made the poor, overworked peasants radiate with joy, yelling and chanting. Everything, they knew, would eventually be ok again- because these soldiers would fight for them and guard all they held dear. With men such as these, no one would ever have to worry about living in fear.

And as long as this was the case, Jovan would continue to fight, everyday. As long as his heart would beat, he would fight. As long as his lungs would breathe, he would fight. As long as the sparrows would fly through the trees and the ocean raged on, he would fight.

Armor would grace his body, and a prosperous journey would ensue. Because no matter how much he sometimes would regret what would come of the battles, he would always find himself going out to do what he did best.

So, for these reasons, he would go to the banquet and celebrate.

Jovan took a deep breath as he sat on his bed and stared at his dress shirt, hanging on the door of his wardrobe beside the bed. So much pageantry it had been a part of, and so much confidence it had given him. Tonight was different- because he had faced some of the things that had troubled his heart the most. Nothing would ever change the events that had transpired; but with time, he knew that he would be strong enough to overcome it.

He wondered if his heart would ever love again. He wondered if he were now damaged by the amount of love he had given up. For a person that had never shown his emotion and never got close to anyone, he had fallen fast for her, and he had loved her with all the love he could give someone. He would have died for her, he would have rather had her than anything else in this world. And though her love had been fleeting, his would be eternal. He would feel saddened when he would think of her, because she had been his true love lost. But he was glad he got to feel the intensity of true love. It had made him feel so alive, it had made him see that there were beautiful parts of this horrendous earth.

He hardly recognized himself from the man he had been a few weeks ago. Then, he had been a rage-fueled, testosterone-driven, enamored soldier, that had been angry at so many things. Now he had an understanding with the man he shared green eyes with, he knew the truth behind his fellow knight that had been his enemy; he knew what it was like to hold his soul mate and feel her heart beating. He knew the nature of his old friend River, and he knew how she desired him so, and he knew how though her exterior was surreal, her heart was impure.

For the first time in a long time Jovan slept that night. Samuel was still dead, and the well-being of the kingdom still hang from his shoulders. But he knew that when he awakened, he would be honored and praised, the women would come to him and the king would appreciate him. Once he was in a ball room surrounded by beautiful people and beautiful things, he would be reminded of why he did what he did. No matter what, Jovan's legacy would never change.

Nothing Jovan had done would be erased from this earth. All the people from towns over knew of his legacy, they knew of his valor, they knew of his skill and his strength. The women knew of his chiseled body and his heartbreak smile, his emerald eyes and the way his blonde hair would fall over one eye, as he would push it behind his ear with a callused hand. The men knew of his war stories, his fighting and the way he would never back down, even from the face of death; because the crucifix he wore around his neck and on his shield would give him all the faith he needed.

The next day, Jovan woke with more strength than he had than ever before. He had to keep fighting for those that could no longer- like Samuel and his father. As a knight would go about his life, he would always feel the need to give up; but each time, he would come across another reason to keep going. Each time, he would become wiser and stronger and a much better version of himself.

Jovan had always been hard on himself- but he never once had any doubt. He never for one second thought he was not good enough.

The blood, sweat, and tears he had put into this place had rewarded him in ways he could not explain. He would love it if the world would stand still before him, and maybe then he could look across the people and the town, and see what he had done. He had left his mark on this town- it had used him up and spat him out. But he found himself humbled by it, and no war or enemy would ever take away the honor his spirit possessed. The way he was before and the way he had become was so different, but it was not night and day.

It was like sunset.

When sleep would find him, he would dream; and when he dreamt, he remembered. Things that shaped him and moved him and made him feel would always remind him of what he used to be and why he fought the way he did.

As Jovan put on his silk shirt, he knew one thing for sure: he is changing. His world from before is now gone. His past is behind him; his wounds are healed. His words are not forgotten.

His hands go weak when he touches the one he loves; his body goes weak when he faces the truth. He is not a prisoner to the things of the world, but instead desires to seek a higher understanding. His muscles and his mind work together to fight his battles and he will never turn away.

He wakes up to light and shuns darkness.

He holds onto love with all that he has. He gives himself to things that matter most, and his valor will live on forever- in the hearts of his men, in the town he fights for, and in his strong, beating heart.

He is never looking back. This is his metamorphosis.

This is his Renaissance.